SEEING FOREVER

SEEING FOREVER

ROBERT J. MCCARTER

Little Hummingbird Publishing

Cover image © Ig0rzh | Dreamstime.com

Version 1.0, April 2018

ISBN: 978-1-941153-01-7

Visit Robert's website at: RobertJMcCarter.com

Published by:

Little Hummingbird Publishing

P.O. Box 23518

Flagstaff, AZ 86002

www.LittleHummingbird.com

Little Hummingbird Publishing is a division of Arapas, Inc. Find more about Arapas at: www.Arapas.com.

❀ Created with Vellum

For my forever friend John

Chapter One

AS I ENTERED THE WORLD, I WAS OF A MIND TO END IT ALL. What was left for me? I should at least place myself in suspend for a good long while—a century or two. I was young when the idea of immortality had captured me. I had no idea what I was in for. How could I?

This world was named "Home" and housed many consciousnesses. After my last, long suspension, that had attracted my attention. It was also taking up half of our system's resources. The two had been enough to turn me away from the Erase program. To try one last time to find something, some reason to continue this existence. Anything.

I stood there blinking in the bright sun like some novice waking up for the first time. It was late summer, hot with a gentle breeze playing with my short hair. The grass was green and well manicured—but thankfully, not perfect—hills of it rolling towards the ocean. The air had that seaside tang, and I caught the scent of sweet flowers that I couldn't quite identify.

I was in the arrival circle, a red circle painted on weathered cobblestone. Two old men sat nearby playing chess under a big maple tree, but ignored me, as is protocol. A boy was dangling up in the branches of an oak tree, a smile wide on his freckle-strewn face, his mother looking on in dismay.

I almost left then. Just a thought while in the circle and I would be gone, back to Level One where I could suspend or choose another world. Where I could end it, if I finally had the courage to run the Erase program. It was the boy that set me on edge. I had done that, of course, we all had done it. Entered a world as a child and "grown up" again. But the idea repulsed me now and I didn't know if I wanted to be on a world where the oldest of souls pretended to be children. It's not right.

I took a deep breath and let out a long sigh. My mood was so heavy I could taste it—a sour, moldy flavor that was unpleasant, but given my mood, accurate.

But I was here, might as well at least take a walk. I looked myself over. I was wearing a blue bathing suit, flip-flops, and a casual, off-white button-down shirt. Beachwear. Everything looked good, I had rendered well. Not that anyone rendered poorly anymore. I was showing my age again.

Another breath and I stepped out of the circle. The two old men didn't even look up. The freckly kid had jumped down and was climbing another tree, the dutiful mother keeping an eye on him. I walked down the cobblestoned path, quickly past them, and headed towards the ocean.

As I walked through the trees and came out onto the vast sloping lawn, it became apparent that the beach was below and that the park ended in a cliff. The path teed and wound along the cliff with benches made of iron and wood, placed at regular intervals.

To my left, several hundred yards away, I could see that there were stairs built into the cliff—a winding affair that led to the beach. There were plenty of souls down there, playing in the surf, lounging in the sun, walking slowly on the sand. The fishy, seaweedy smell of the ocean was strong and the breeze stiff. I wrinkled my nose. I was not fond of oceans or their unrelenting wetness and smell.

"Would you like to talk about it?"

I turned and saw him standing there. He looked to be in his mid-thirties and had on loose cotton pants the color of sand and a flowing white shirt. I didn't recognize him, even though I must have met him somewhere along the journey. Maybe I had forgotten. Maybe he had a different face.

I shrugged, letting his blue eyes capture mine briefly. Even though his face didn't seem familiar, those eyes did. I turned back to the ocean. I hadn't spoken to anyone in so long I felt unaccountably shy.

"I'm a good listener," he offered.

I looked back at him. His face wasn't perfect, his chin a bit too square, his eyes a tad too far apart. It was a normal face and I liked that about him.

"You are kind," I said. It seemed a good phrase to end my long silence with.

He returned a compassionate smile, showing less than perfect teeth. "Sometimes it helps to talk about it."

I nodded and took a deep breath, letting the seaside air fill my lungs. The air was too moist for my liking, but it felt good to take a deep breath.

"You know who I am," I said.

He nodded even though it wasn't a question. Everyone knew who I was. I was the oldest, how could they not know me? "Pretend I don't," he said.

I smiled, it was a small, fleeting thing, like youth or innocence or even life itself. He was offering me a new game, and that didn't happen often enough.

"My name is Paul," I said, extending my hand. "Paul Cruz."

"Simon," he said, clasping my hand. His grip was strong and his hand rough.

So we found a bench and I told him all about it.

Initially the words came slowly, like a shy girl on her first date. But it did feel good to talk about it, and then the words came faster, the story spinning forth like that shy girl telling her closest friends about that first date.

Chapter Two

My wife, Viola, hated the idea.

This was back in the twenty-second century when Earth was just recovering from the Shift. Water levels had risen. Populations had shifted. Disease and disaster had made a large dent in the population, and bitter wars had been fought. I was lucky to be born after all that, but the world still had the flavor of desperation. Things were finally getting better, but no one could really admit it yet.

When we met, Viola was twenty and I was nineteen. We met at university in Texas, and it was a torrid thing—biology driving us to propagate the species.

But no, I am being too cynical. She was young and beautiful with gorgeous brown hair that flowed in sheets around her shoulders and laughing green eyes. She was smart at times. Serious at others. And she tasted like life to me. I couldn't get enough of her for those first few years, and she couldn't get enough of me.

We married. Had children. Worked too much. Grew old. The usual.

The day I told her what I wanted to do was on my sixtieth birthday. We had spent the last year in Australia—they had survived the Shift better than most, having always had a small population given their land mass, and we found ourselves spending more and more time there. The Outback was something I had grown to love with its dry expanses of wild desert.

We had left the comfort of our cabin and taken a hike up a hill nearby. It afforded us a dramatic view of the desert—rust colored sand tentatively held together by scraggly, but hearty, bushes sweeping down as far as the eye could see.

I remember the hot sun, the smell of our sweat, the sound of our breathing. I remember the contortions her face went through when I told her about the Osiris Corporation, about what they could do, that I wanted to sign up. First confusion, then shock, and then disappointment.

"But, why? Why would you want to do that?" Viola asked. Her green eyes weren't laughing, but she still had that gorgeous long hair, strands of it waving in the trickle of a breeze.

This was delicate territory for us. When I met her, she had a passing relationship with religion, as did I. We were both acquainted with religion, at times interested, and at others repelled, but not true believers or anything. As the decades had passed, our feelings had diverged. She believed more and more. I believed less and less.

I shrugged. "It seems like a grand adventure," I said, "life beyond the biological, escaping the infirmities of this 'mortal coil.'"

Her face puckered, making her look more her age. "Maybe

if you'd just come to church, Paul. Just listen to Pastor Franks. Just give it a chance."

And there we were in that rut of ours, and on my birthday.

"The singularity is here," I said. "Our consciousnesses can be transferred from a delicate biological housing to a hearty technological one. I'm signing up. If I do it soon, they'll include free upgrades for the first fifty years."

"Singularity? Are we talking about black holes and one-dimensional points now?" She knew how I was using the term; this was her way of stalling, processing.

"Not black holes. The term is used in mathematics, technology, and yes, astronomy, to describe a point where things become unpredictable and growth becomes exponential. We're at that point with technology."

She sighed and her face fell, and I was relieved it wasn't going to be a fight. But when I saw the fear that blossomed there I would have preferred the fight. "When?" she asked. "You are young still. You are not doing this now, are you?"

The religious had taken to calling it a mortal sin. And I guess, from their perspective, I can see their point.

The machines learn all they can about your brain, your body, and everything in between. Months of scans, legions of tests, endless poking and prodding, then when you are close to death—and aye, here's the rub—but not dead, they put you under, they stop your biological functions, they take your brain apart a cell at a time, mapping each and every neuron. They sample your organs, study your skeletal and muscular system, hell, they even map all the microbes that are part of you, your microbiome.

All of that is combined with all the data from the tests while your biology was still functional. And then *poof*. You wake up, your consciousness running on a machine. You are alive, but no longer biological.

It's a strange term, singularity. In a technological sense it originally referred to the point where computers and AI got so good that improvements became extremely rapid, resulting in an explosion of technology, and computers becoming smarter than humans. Practically, though, it referred to the point when computers were powerful enough to house a human consciousness. Not "artificial" in terms of the intelligence, just a different platform for it. The point when humans transcended biology and merged with technology. It's why we call ourselves Singulars.

I smiled, taking her face in my hands. I loved her still, not in that torrid way of our meeting, but in a wider and gentler way. "You're stuck with this bag of bones for quite some time, my dear."

She sniffed and nodded. We didn't speak of it again, but it cast a shadow on the rest of our marriage.

———

THE CRYING OF A SEAGULL BROUGHT ME BACK TO THE OCEAN and the bench and Simon. Someone was walking into the ocean, reaching down and pulling up clams, cracking them open and throwing the meat up in the air. The gulls wheeled and dove, snatching them out of the air, some crying with delight, some with frustration.

"This was very early on?" Simon asked. He sat very comfortably with his legs crossed, leaning slightly towards me. He had told the truth, he was a good listener.

"I bought into the first offering," I said. "I was wealthy, you had to be then, and it took a big chunk of our net worth to do it. But…" I trailed off, watching the woman feeding the gulls, becoming mesmerized by their acrobatic flight.

Simon didn't push, he sat there watching the gulls with me as the waves crashed, the children played, and the adults lounged down on the beach.

"My father was an investor," I finally said. "He didn't build anything, just moved money around. He had a nose for it in those turbulent times. A lot of wealth is created in wars, in economic collapses, and certainly during the chaos of the Shift. My parents had me late—they were about fifty when I was born. They had been born into the early chaos of the Shift and had survived the worst of it. My father taught me to see change right before it came, to leap on opportunity, to always strive to reduce risk.

"And that's what I was doing. I was unsure of eternity, so in signing up for 'life beyond the biological,' as the ads then said, I was reducing risk."

Simon nodded. "And the wars, the Shift, they were catalytic in the development of the tech?"

I nodded. "People started talking about the technological singularity, about human consciences on a technological platform, at the end of the twentieth century, but it took a lot longer than they expected. Most of the tech was developed for WWW—World War Water. First getting better with robotic prosthetics all those soldiers needed. When they put chips in their heads so they could control their new limbs, they had to learn a lot about the brain. Then when the humans left the battlefield and the drones and robots took over, we had to get a lot better at making machines think. The bulk of their intelligence had to be self-contained, and that gave us yet another reason to understand the brain better.

"But progress didn't happen until the wars ended and peace came. Humans were living longer, but never long enough. The tech was almost there. The singularity was inevitable."

The woman had stopped feeding the gulls down on the beach. Their cries had a lamenting quality to them as they slowly flew above her hoping for more.

The words "never long enough" echoed through my head, sounding very much like the cries of those seagulls. I used to believe that there could never be enough life. I was no longer sure. Not at all.

———

VIOLA STAYED FOR ANOTHER FIVE YEARS AND THEN SHE divorced me. It was the belief gap that did it. She believed in a mythical god that would take care of her immortal soul if she obeyed the proper rituals and acquiesced to its bizarre demands. I didn't believe in god and had, in fact, set my course to what was becoming thought of in the religious community as the greatest sin of all—eternal life without god's intercession.

The divorce was bitter and took most of my remaining wealth. But that didn't really bother me. I had the lessons my father taught me. I saw opportunities, I seized them, my wealth came back and then grew. I was alone. I didn't have the energy or desire to find another partner. I had little else to do but make money.

On my ninetieth birthday, I was back in Australia. I got

word from my grandson that Viola had died. The coastlines were well stabilized by then and I was staying at an exclusive beachside resort on the Gold Coast. I remember stumbling out of my cabana and onto the beach, walking into the waves. I was weeping. I couldn't stop. We had been apart for twenty-five years, but she had been the love of my life. I felt something tear in me, deep down. I felt alone and unmoored. I felt scared.

Viola had believed—and if she was right, she was in heaven. I was in the water up to my chest, the waves crashing over my head, salt water stinging my eyes and getting in my mouth, my cries of grief drowned out by the eternal roar of the ocean.

It was dark, a moonless night. The stars arrayed above me, making me feel all that much more alone.

I had been getting my checkups with the Osiris Corporation twice a year. They were making sure I was healthy, looking for signs of mental degradation. You definitely want to make the "transition"—nice euphemism, huh?—before senility or dementia hits. I was taking my anti-aging meds, eating the right foods in the right amounts, exercising religiously. My body was strong, my mind clear. I was still healthy.

When I crawled out of the ocean, I don't know how long later, I called them right up. I scheduled the transition. With Viola gone, I was done with this biological life.

Chapter Three

"I HAVE MY AFTERLIFE," I SAID TO SIMON, GESTURING AT THE beach tableau below us. "She has hers." I stopped and stared at the ocean, feeling the strength of that memory. Of the salt water in my hair and my eyes. The pounding of my heart. The fear I felt when I decided to transition. "Want to know something funny?"

Simon nodded and leaned closer.

"That day, when I got the news, I hoped that she was right. That she had gone to heaven and that I was about to commit a mortal sin. With all my heart, I hoped she was right."

"And now?" he asked.

I shrugged. "I still hope she was right, for her sake I do." Simon had this look of compassion on his face, a softness that was compelling, so I said more than I would have. "That hope is for my own sake, too." One eyebrow raised on his face. "I feel better hoping that the spark of consciousness that was her wasn't snuffed out when she died."

Simon nodded.

"I hope… but I don't believe, and I doubt it. I did that day. I do today. So I made the appointment, I took six months to tie up loose ends, say goodbye. I made the 'transition.'"

———

"This is your last chance to abort," the woman said. I am embarrassed to say that I don't remember her name, but I remember her face. Blue eyes, high cheekbones, thick lips. As I stared up at her face from the operating room table, I remember thinking that she was much too attractive to be a doctor. But she had probably bought that face with the money she made helping people transition.

Her hair was blond, stuffed under one of those surgical hairnets. She had lipstick on in a lighter shade of red. Her face would be the last thing I would ever see as a human being. The last thing.

I drank it in, blinking slowly. My mouth was dry and the operating table felt cold underneath me. I could hear the whispers of others in the operating room, but I only saw her.

"Mr. Cruz," she said, a small smile on her beautiful lips. "Paul. I need you to confirm you want to do this or we will abort."

I nodded, just barely, moving my restrained head as far as it would go. Not in assent, just to acknowledge that I had heard her. The money I had spent for my spot was non-refundable. It was probably more profitable for me to abort, which could explain the dramatic operating room last-chance-to-abort question.

"I need you to say yes or no," she said.

God, she was beautiful. I wanted to touch her face. Not in a sexual way, but just to make sure she was real. I felt a tear make an escape from my left eye and trickle down to the table below me.

"Can... can you just... touch me?" I asked. My head was locked in a metal contraption, my arms and legs strapped down. I couldn't move.

She licked her lips, her blue eyes widening and then she smiled. Just a tiny smile. Just a brief smile. But it made me feel warm inside.

She leaned closer, her finger catching another renegade tear as it trickled out. I wondered how many of us are like this on her table. I had met her briefly while I was still being prepped. Her blue scrubs could not hide her sensuous curves. She wasn't anything like my Viola, whose beauty had been much more subtle.

"It's okay, Paul," she whispered in my ear. I could feel the tickle of her warm breath and smell the scent of oranges. "I promise you that we are very good at this now. You will wake up and feel just like you."

She lied to me, of course. With that beautiful face and that sensuous body, she lied. Viola would have looked on her as a temptress, leading me away from the path of righteousness.

I told her to do it. She told me to start counting backwards from one hundred.

I got to ninety-two before I was out.

————

"When did you transition?" I asked Simon. I was buying time away from my story. I needed to surface and smell the clean air, hear the roar of the surf, do something besides be in my past.

"Fourth wave," he said.

That explained some things. I had been much less social since the end of the second wave. "Mars?" I asked.

He nodded. "After the revolution. It was a much easier decision then."

"How old were you?" I asked.

"Thirty-six," he said. "Perfectly healthy."

I felt my belly tighten at the thought. I had transitioned when I was an old man in grief. He had done it as a very young man in good health. Things had changed so much from the beginning.

"Why did you do it?" I asked.

"Just reducing risk," he said with a smile, playfully echoing my reason. "No. Actually, I did it for the adventure of it. Infinite worlds in here to explore. New worlds out there to discover." He gestured up towards the sun which had made noticeable progress towards the ocean.

He was referring to the vessels that carried our consciousness outwards towards Alpha Centauri.

We sat quietly for a time as I breathed deeply of the salt air, felt the warm rays of the sun on my face, and heard the cries of children playing floating up from below.

The "worlds" were not real. Not biologically at least. They were constructs made of the same stuff our consciousnesses were made of. Electrons. Transistors. Software.

But it felt real, at least it did now. Back when that beautiful woman with the blue eyes and wonderful lips—my devil-doctor—had lied to me, it was not like this. Not like this at all.

Chapter Four

I JOLTED BACK TO CONSCIOUSNESS, AFRAID. SOMETHING WASN'T right. I was in danger. Where was I?

I couldn't see. I couldn't hear. I couldn't feel or taste or smell. I was awake in a void. Floating alone, without sensation or orientation. I "was," but I didn't know what I was. No body. No senses. No nothing. Just a mind afloat in a void.

You will wake up and feel just like you. Hardly.

The void was a vice around me and my mind desperately tried to escape. Except there was no escape, there was no comfort, there was nothing. Just my mind adrift in a vast emptiness.

I don't know how long it lasted, time wasn't anything I could measure. It felt like days at least, or maybe years. For that time, I wasn't sane. My mind kept reaching out trying to feel, to sense, to know. And it couldn't. At first my thoughts were rational—I remembered that I had been in an operating room, that I was having my consciousness transferred. I figured there was a small problem, that things would make sense shortly.

And then my mind slipped away from me and I was just terrified. Those rational thoughts would occur, but in the middle of them they would just disappear and I would only be left with a gasping desperate need.

Alone suddenly took on a whole new definition, as did terrified. A consciousness completely untethered is nothing but fear itself.

It did change, though. Eventually.

Sound first. A wash of hissing white noise, like static from an old-fashioned analog radio. No data, just noise.

Who's there? I thought, but the hissing noise didn't answer. It got louder, painfully loud, and then it was gone. Once it was gone, I wished it would come back.

Then came light. Sparks of white in the void like stars winking on and off many light years away. A flicker, a flash, but it didn't last long. Even as ephemeral as this light was, it helped. It gave my mind something to do. *What was that light? Maybe there is something out there after all. Will it ever come back? Oh, there's another one. That one's tinged with red on the edge. Red... I love the color red. Oh, there's a yellow one, yellow like a banana or the sun.*

The isolation had reduced me to being a child. I grabbed on to any sensation and held it tightly.

The hissing noise started again, and the lights went away. Except this time the noise wasn't a uniform hiss, but was rising and falling. Wait. That sounded like "Paul."

This went on for a long time. Noise that sounded vaguely like something that would be replaced by flashing pinpricks of light in various hues. The lights started to look like something—a tan shaded oval, two blue orbs with a slash of red below. But I couldn't make it out.

The sound became more and more frustrating. Words were being said, but I just couldn't understand them. Something was wrong, very wrong. I wanted to die then. For real. I wanted a cessation of consciousness. Not the void I had woken to, not these unfathomable lights and sounds, but nothing. Truly nothing.

Viola had longed for the embrace of a god. Right then I wanted to just not be. Done. Gone. Dead.

My ability to see, to hear, was that of a newborn baby, but my mind was that of an old man. I had senses, but I could make no sense of their input. Nothing went together. I had gone to sleep sane and woken to the incomprehensible and the terrifying. I was lost. I was alone. I was imprisoned in my mind.

I was pleading for the end as the lights and the sound started doing their dance of frustration together. But who was I pleading to? A force outside myself, a force stronger than me? Was I praying for an end? Was I beseeching a god I didn't believe in?

I laughed. Well, in my mind I did. I wasn't making any sound—that I could detect—but the wave of mirth bounced around my consciousness, and I felt (even though I couldn't feel) lighter. I was buoyed by the humor, my very spirits lifting. "Spirits" lifting. That sent out new waves of ironic humor. A spirit implied an afterlife—a spiritual one, not the hellish technological one I was trapped in.

My mind burned with the humor of it, the irony of it, the joy of it. These were just thoughts, and except for the confusing sensory data, I was completely locked in my head, but I learned something very important then. I learned how to survive. How to be just a mind and still be a little bit sane. How to have nothing but thought and memory and be okay.

I tuned out the sound and lights, which I was surprised I could do. They were still there, I just didn't give them my attention. I focused on humor. I started remembering jokes, really bad jokes, and running them through my mind. Word play, surprising endings, putting human fallibility into fine relief.

I found my memory to be excellent. I summoned up jokes with ease. Everything from stupid puns (Age is important only if you're cheese or wine) to bawdy limericks (there once was man from Nantucket...). Many of them fell flat on the stage of my mind, but some of them amused me greatly.

And then when I had run through my repertoire of jokes, I started making things up. Silly things. *Knock, knock. Who's there? Consciousness. Consciousness who? Consciousness called, it wants its sanity back.*

Silly or stupid, rude or nonsensical, I would ride the wave of humor as long as I could and then find something else.

Until...

"Paul? Can you hear me? Paul?"

It was the husky voice of the blond temptress doctor. The last thing I saw as a Biological was her face. The first thing I heard as a Non-Biological—as a Singular—was her voice. It was relatively deep for a woman's voice with a rough edge to it. It was a sexy voice, the kind that you would like to hear quiet and low on the pillow next to you after a night of debauchery.

I wanted to reply, but I didn't know how to speak. I had no body, no lungs, no diaphragm, no vocal cords to vibrate. How the hell was I supposed to speak? My humor vanished and I began to panic.

"Just stay calm, Paul. I'm right here. I won't leave you."

She's the devil. The thought just leaked out, coherent and clear. *I'm in hell and she's the devil.* I felt ashamed of the thought. First, I knew it to not be true—intellectually speaking—but emotionally, oh yeah, that's what she was at that point. And, second, here I was again with theist thoughts leaking into my technological afterlife.

Husky laughter bounced around my consciousness. "I can assure you that I am not the devil," she said.

Yes, you are, but a damn sexy one, I thought before I realized what was happening

"Well, that compliment, I will take."

The lights had become coherent. I was looking at the lovely face of my devil-doctor. She wasn't dressed in scrubs anymore, her long flaxen hair flowing around her shoulders. She had a white blouse on, revealing a fair amount of cleavage. I could see her clearly, and I mean *clearly*. I could see each and every pore. I could see the dark band around her blue irises. I could see the slight throb of a vein on her temple. She was all I could "see." No background, none that I could sense. Just her face and her voice. That was it. She was my world.

She may have been my devil, but I clung to her with a fierceness born out of necessity.

Chapter Five

THE CLIFF WASN'T SHEER, WHICH I LIKED ABOUT THIS WORLD. Many of the first worlds were all extremes—the highest mountains, the sheerest cliffs, the deepest ocean, the most beautiful of people. The extremes had gotten tiresome. If everything was THE BEST, then nothing was.

This cliff was very steep, but not sheer. It broke away in stages with narrow ledges on the way down with viney green plants growing on them. As I stared down, my flip-flopped feet right on the edge, I saw a small grey bird picking at the first little ledge, hopping from place to place, its beak diving past the foliage to get to the ground.

"What happens if I jump?" I said quietly. Simon was behind me, still sitting on the bench. Last I looked he was at ease, leaning back casually, one leg crossed over the other.

"The world will stop you, if it can," he said, calmly, like we were discussing the most mundane of things. And, I guess, in many ways we were. "A sudden breeze, a person passing by and steadying you. You know the kind of thing."

"What if the world can't stop me?"

"Then you will have a realistic, and painful, fall. Your body will probably die on those rocks down there."

At the bottom were large lumps of black rocks sitting in the sand about two hundred feet below. A body would fall, would bounce, would land on those rocks. I leaned back just a bit. "What is the realism grade here?" I asked.

I heard Simon stand and let out a gentle sigh. I heard his feet on the grass and then I felt the warmth of him next to me. "Level Ten," he said.

I blinked and took a step back. Level Ten is biological norm. You get tired, you get sore, you get hungry and horny and sick. At first there had been lots of low-level worlds where you could fly, where you couldn't die, where you had a body, but things weren't quite "real." In the beginning the tech wasn't good enough to make a truly realistic world. And then, later on, we were all busy exploring worlds as Non-Biologicals (on one world you could be the wind) or as animals (I spent several lifetimes soaring as an eagle) or as mere concepts (you could be heat on one world). This was the first Level Ten world that I knew about—even Hugh found creating Level Ten a challenge.

Simon's words made me more aware of my body. I felt an uncomfortable tensing in my stomach, slightly painful. As if on cue, it made an audible rumble.

"Sounds like you're hungry," Simon said.

I nodded, my brows furrowed. It had been so long that the sensation was surprising and felt very strong.

"There's a little place down the beach," he said, his hand

pointing to the stairs that wound their way down the cliff. "Fish tacos, best in town."

I nodded, but didn't speak. He led the way.

The stairs were made of wood, and up close I could see that some of the white paint was peeling, the relentless wind and moisture talking their toll. They creaked as we walked down them, and I could smell the musty scent of wood beginning to rot. More Level Ten details.

When we got down to the beach, the sun was turning a bit orange as it approached the ocean. It was the right size and right color, its warm rays kissing my face. An earth-like sun. This was an earth-like beach. Most of the families had gone. I saw a few couples walking hand in hand dressed in bathing suits or loose clothing, the breeze playing with their clothes or their hair.

"We all work here," Simon told me as he walked down the beach a pace in front of me. He had taken his shoes off and carried them in one hand. "There are not enough of us for a true economy, so a lot of goods are created by the world for us, but everyone of age has a place, has a job."

"What is your job?" I asked.

He turned, smiled at me, the thin lines around his eyes crinkling up. He was aging here. Those lines would grow deeper until he was like those old men playing chess by the arrival circle. "I am part of the 'Welcome Wagon.'"

The phrase was one I didn't know. Welcome Wagon. I held the question in my mind and waited for the definition to flow in as a gentle whisper, but it didn't. I stopped, my feet on the warm sand, the taste of salt in my mouth. That wasn't right. I had access to the whole of human knowledge, why didn't I know what a "Welcome Wagon" was?

"I don't know what that means," I said.

Simon was a few paces ahead of me. He stopped and looked back at me, shielding his eyes from the sun. "It's a term from the mid-twentieth century. When someone moved into a neighborhood, a representative would come and greet them. Tell them about the town. Give them maps and gifts from the local businesses. Make them feel welcome."

I nodded. Level Ten. Human norm. That's why I couldn't tap into the larger knowledgebase, I only knew what I knew. I suddenly felt naked, exposed.

Why were people living this way now? I know I had spent a lot of time in suspend. I had expected changes, but not like this.

"What brought you to our world?" Simon asked.

I shrugged. "Over thirty percent of the Singulars are here now and the majority of our processing resources. I was curious." I hadn't seen such a concentration for decades, not since the beginning.

"Come on," Simon said with a wave. "You must be starved by now, and I am sure you have a lot of questions."

Chapter Six

LEVEL ZERO. THAT IS WHERE I WAS WITH MY BEAUTIFUL DEVIL-doctor. Where I woke up. Where I felt anything but "just like me."

Level Zero. The place where a consciousness always is after booting up or a reset.

Level Zero. The only place Singulars had for the first twenty years.

That's why a lot of us were lost in the beginning. Level Zero is not even a room, you don't have a "body" so you can't be in a "room." You can see and hear, that's it. But it is not like seeing and hearing as a Biological. You have no eyes, you can't move your head. What you see is what you see. What you hear is what you hear. Raw input. No control.

These days Level Zero is a brief moment while your system boots up and then you are at Level One, where you at least have a body. But back then, it wasn't like that. I spent what seemed like years in Level Zero.

"You lied to me," I said to her. Her face loomed large in my vision. I was getting comfortable with Level Zero. I could control when I "spoke" now. It was the louder thoughts that came through clearly to an Operator like her.

"Yes, I did," she said with a red-lipped smile. She could see, in intimate detail, what was going on in my head. She could suspend me, reboot me, blind me, or make me deaf with the touch of a button. I was afraid, but I had begun to get tired of this.

"This is not what I expected it to be. I am not just like myself as you promised." I knew she knew what I was speaking about, but I felt the need to elaborate.

Her smile was a tight, little thing. I was tired of her. She was tired of me. I had become aware that a lot of time had passed. She was always there, always with me from my perspective, but from her perspective we did this a few hours a day. I was suspended when she wasn't available. It had been six months since the "transfer." I wanted more. But this was a "tricky process." She had told me that many times.

"It will be," she said. "Soon. I promise."

I snorted. Her promises held no weight with me. The image of her stuttered and she was suddenly wearing a blue blouse instead of a green one. I checked the system time and she had suspended me for a week.

"What is going on, I—" I began.

She held up her hand, cutting me off. "It's time," she said.

"Time for what?"

"Level One."

And then everything changed. I had a sense of space, a grey floor, white walls, a large screen on one wall with the doctor's smiling face on it. I had hands and legs and feet. They were smooth, simple, lacking the complexity of a real hand or a real leg, but they were there. I was dressed in a seamless grey jumpsuit. I patted my hand against my chest and I felt… something. Not much, but after all that time at Level Zero, feeling anything was a joy. I laughed out loud, so happy to feel a little bit real.

"This is just the beginning," she said. "Come over here and let me give you a tour."

———

THE RESTAURANT THAT SIMON LED ME TO WAS MORE OF A shack nestled up against the cliff. It had a corrugated metal roof held up by brightly painted telephone poles. Round tables were arrayed around it, some in the sun, some under the roof. A smiling round-faced man—looking like he was from Hawaii—greeted us from behind a grill. The smell of cooking fish and vegetables was heavenly and made my stomach flip with joy.

Simon led me to a table out in the sun and we sat. I took off my flip-flops and dug my feet into the warm sand.

"It was rough in the beginning," he said.

I nodded. "Level One was a relief at first, but it wasn't enough. I could communicate with the outside world, manage my affairs, watch movies, read, but it became old quick. Cabin fever set in."

"And your devil-doctor?"

"Last time I saw her," I said. "Her job was done and she moved on."

"Here you go, boys," the round-faced man said as he set down paper-lined baskets filled with fish tacos and two beers with limes sticking out the top. The heavenly smell of them made my mouth water. The big man swept back to his grill and left the two of us alone.

We ate in silence. I took my time, chewing slowly, savoring the textures and the flavors. When I had been biological, I had wolfed things down. Eating was something to get done so I could move on to more important things. Not now. Being able to eat, to feel the growing warmth in my belly, to feel my body relax around the food, was a treat.

It's not lost on me that the experience is illusory. That I don't have a "body," that all of this is "simulated." But that doesn't reduce the pleasure. In some ways it intensifies it.

When my hunger was sated, I took a pull on the cold beer and watched the sun sink down into the ocean. The round-faced man was lighting tiki torches, the sharp smell of burning kerosene and smoke adding to the ambience.

"So what are you all doing here?" I asked.

Simon leaned forward, his blue-eyed gaze intense, a small smile playing on his lips. "We're *living*."

"But, Level Ten. Why Level Ten? Wouldn't Nine be better, a little less constrained by 'biology.'" I stifled a yawn. Now that my belly was full I was beginning to get sleepy, the beer contributing.

Simon took a deep breath and slowly let it out. "This is the kind of world we were designed for. We're trying it out, seeing what happens. Our belief is that we will thrive here." He pulled out what looked like a cell phone and pushed it across the table towards me. "I am going to leave you now. This will—"

"What?" I said, cutting him off. I had grown accustomed to

Simon's calm presence. Those blue eyes of his set me at ease. I didn't know if I wanted to be alone.

His smile relaxed me. "I've booked you a room at the hotel. It's just down the beach." He pointed to a one-story structure built back against the cliff a few hundred yards away. Lights were coming on as the sky darkened. "Take your time. Explore. Get some sleep. I'll meet you in the morning and maybe you can tell me about the revolution."

He stood and extended his hand. I stood up and shook it. I didn't know Simon at all. All I knew was that he was kind and a good listener. "I'll be by around breakfast time. If you need anything, just use the phone."

With that he walked away. The big Hawaiian man came by, took our plates and left me with another beer.

Level Ten. Human norm. I didn't know if I was going to like it, but it intrigued me. After being alive for so long—biological and otherwise—it felt good to be intrigued.

Chapter Seven

THE REVOLUTION. WHERE DO I BEGIN?

I've described the beginning of my journey as a Singular. It got off to a rough start and really didn't get much better.

Well, as new levels became available, each one was a relief. Level Two and my form and the room got a bit more detailed. Motor control was terrible—I lurched around like Frankenstein's Monster—but at least I had a body. Level Three and a rudimentary sense of smell was introduced. Level Four and the worlds started to expand and we Singulars could meet together and interact. It wasn't very close to being human, but for many us it had been so long that the substitute was a relief.

Actually, I should back up. In the beginning of all this, back when I had been sixty and signed the contract, there were souls entering the singularity. Rich, old men and women desperate to hold on to consciousness no matter the form (and that does describe all of us in the first wave).

Back then the technology was new and exciting, but much less mature than when I came in. It took me six months to get to Level One. At the time, this was uncommon—something about how my brain was wired—back then six months was short. It took a year or two for some of the early Singulars.

Most of them went mad before then. Most of them were permanently suspended. Many deleted when obscure clauses in their contracts were invoked.

After Viola divorced me and during the several decades before she died, she would send me each and every article about the difficulty of the technology. It was her way of asking whether I was sure. She didn't need to send them along, I was watching it closely. Progress was difficult and sporadic at first, but it steadily got better.

But, really, nothing was that livable until Level Four worlds came into existence. Many consciousnesses were damaged, some severely, during that time. Back before the revolution, back when our servers were still Earth-bound, you would see the damaged ones wandering through the worlds. They were crazy in one way or another. Worlds were created just for them to wander through, ghost worlds that no one else visited. The ones that were too far gone to function were permanently suspended.

But I am talking about the revolution now. It started like many do, as a disagreement over resources. In this case money.

I was an early adopter and my contract included fifty years of free upgrades. And while I received those upgrades, they were very slow in coming and often delayed for nonsensical reasons. Several times I had to file lawsuits to get things moving.

This wasn't a big deal, and wasn't that unexpected, but it highlighted the fact that the process, technology, and software was all owned by a single company. The Osiris Corporation. We Singulars were their clients.

And just as all public corporations do, they were trying to maximize their profit for their stockholders.

But their clients were consciousnesses and Osiris held the keys to their very existence in their hands.

And our legal status was very much in question.

Not that we didn't have a legal status. Each one of us Singulars were encased in a corporation which let us operate in the world to a certain degree. I formed my corporation before I was transferred and put all my assets in it. My living descendants were on the board of directors. I structured it so my post-biological self could keep control of it.

But in the outside world, things were more complicated. The religious community hated us. The world entered another recession. Countries fought wars. The flesh and blood lived and died. The only people truly interested in us were our families and those that either hated or misunderstood us.

We became a new, misunderstood minority fighting for our rights which were completely controlled by an outside force.

———

"I HOPE I'M NOT BORING YOU WITH THE HISTORY LESSON," I SAID to Simon.

We were walking along the beach after a nice breakfast at

the hotel. We had passed the cliff and were walking next to rolling hills with small houses placed here and there.

"No. No. Not at all. I know about the revolution, of course. I remember hearing about it when I was on Mars Colony. But hearing it direct from the source... I'm not bored in the least." He ended with a smile.

"Do you give all visitors to this world this much attention?" I asked.

He looked down and then shook his head. "We give each one the attention they need. But no, rarely like this."

We walked in silence; the wind was stronger today, whipping around us and blowing sand against our bodies. It felt scratchy and uncomfortable, just as it should.

There were only a few other people on this long beach. In front of us, a mile or so away, the cliffs returned and a small peninsula jutted out into the ocean. There was a lighthouse perched there.

"So why me?" I asked.

Simon laughed, a brief snort. "You are Paul Cruz. We would love it if you would stay here with us."

I took a deep breath and bit my lip. I stopped walking and held that breath. My body started to protest, screaming for me to let it out, to suck in more oxygen. It worked perfectly, just the way it should. I didn't do it long, just enough to feel that beginning of panic. It was a fine distraction.

While I was enjoying my time with Simon, while I was seeing value in telling my story to him, I wasn't sure I wanted to be here... or anywhere for that matter. With the many years came many losses. Some are too big to let go of, to heal from.

The hotel was nice, but I didn't sleep well there. I kept

waking, memories floating through my head, my existential debate raging. I'm sure they have a pill or something you can take to invoke some system overrides, make you sleep, but I wanted to have the Level Ten experience of a sleepless night. While unpleasant, it had been so long since I had had that experience that it was valuable.

"Are you okay, Paul?" Simon asked. He was standing right next to me—I hadn't noticed him until he spoke. I could smell orange juice on his breath.

I smiled, a bitter play of emotions on my lips. "I'm fine," I told Simon, but it was a lie. I wasn't fine. I didn't know if I wanted to "be" anymore.

It's an odd thought. My Viola knew she was going to die, but believed she would continue to "be." It seems to be something deep in our biology that makes it hard to envision an existence without us as a part of it. But I wasn't biological. I had had consciousness for over one hundred fifty years. I was busy envisioning a world without me.

We walked silently for a time. "So," Simon began, "you started having issues with the Osiris Corporation."

I nodded. "Publicly traded. That was the first problem. Run by Biologicals, that was the second problem."

Chapter Eight

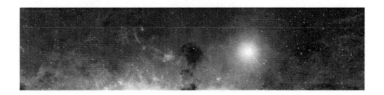

We Singulars talked a lot. We complained about things we didn't like, about the delays and cost in getting to the better worlds. Some of us tried legal action to get what we wanted, some of us complained to our families, and some of us went to the media.

It's that last part that started it all. A Singular named June had a daughter that worked for one of the big media conglomerates. June and her daughter did a glossy exposé on the treatment of Singulars. It went viral.

There was a gamut of reactions from "pull the plug on the sinners," to utter indifference, to the usual jealousy from those that couldn't afford it, to calling our struggle "the new civil rights movement."

It was the last reaction that was new. It was the last reaction that triggered it all. The fuel was there—all the broken promises and exorbitant fees—the reaction to June's story was the spark that ignited it.

The oldest Singular had been in the system for fifty-three years then. Things had progressed, but progressed slowly. In the next three years everything changed.

Actually, at first, nothing really changed. There was the usual media frenzy, the loud opinions for all to hear, and then it got quiet.

We had—quite naively—created a Level Four world to meet in and discuss what was going on. It wasn't much of a world at all. Just a big conference room with lots of arrival circles for Singulars to use to come in and out of the world.

I wasn't all that involved then. My friend Ryan had dragged me along. The story had broken, caused a few waves, and calmed down. Ryan thought I should be there because I had been successful with lawsuits, more successful than some.

Ryan looked like a 1970s' Burt Reynolds—big mustache and full of machismo. This kind of thing was still in vogue. I looked like a 1970s' Harrison Ford, with that lopsided grin of his.

There were lots of other movie stars there too. A few Marilyn Monroes, a Selma Hayek, two different Tom Hanks at different ages, and some modern stars like Angela Cane and Johnson Parker. Everyone had their name floating in the air above them so we all knew who each other was despite our "clothing." It was also customary back then to not alter your voice, but everything else was fair game.

The room was just a big rectangle with a raised stage in the center. There were close to a hundred of us there. This was a large gathering. The total population was around a thousand back then. One by one, those with something to say would stand up there and say it, lead the discussion for a while. The acoustics were perfect so everyone heard what they needed to.

There was a lot of anger and confusion. No one really knew what to do, how to get Osiris to treat us fairly. Things had degraded and there were about fifty different conversations going on at once.

Ryan was telling me—yet again—how he was just about broke and wouldn't be able to afford any more upgrades when the room started to hush. I looked up on the stage and saw June there. She didn't look like a movie star, or even like a young woman. She looked like she did when she transitioned—like a dignified old lady with short silver hair and wrinkled skin. Ryan was still yammering on, so I elbowed him in the ribs and pointed.

"What we have here," she said in her quavering old lady voice, "is a classic asymmetrical power relationship. They are the ones with all the power, we have no power ourselves."

There were a few nods in the audience and a smattering of yeses.

"They have absorbed our consciousnesses into their world and with it most of our wealth." June may have been old and wrinkled, but she had sharp blue eyes and a good mind. Even that far into my post-biological existence it was still so hard not to think in those terms. June looked old so that means certain things and talking like this meant she was a feisty old lady, the kind you listened to, the kind you respected. And maybe that was the brilliance of June keeping her appearance that way. She was an elder. We listened.

"But they messed with the wrong group, didn't they?" June said, standing taller. "Out in the world we were the privileged and the powerful. In here we are..." She paused, a puzzled look on her wrinkled face. "We are nothing but slaves doing what our masters tell us, taking the scraps that they give us."

There were shouts and stomping of feet. June stood taller, her voice getting stronger and louder. "But we know what power feels like, each and every one of us. And we aren't going to lie down and be powerless. No, we are not. We are going to fight back. We are going to get our due. We will not stop talking until Osiris listens. Until we are treated fairly. Until we have what we came for."

I watched. Ryan was pumping his fist up and down. A Marilyn Monroe was jumping into the air in her white dress. Others were shouting or clapping. June stood straight and tall, a grim smile on her face.

This all worried me for the very reason that we *were* powerless, like babes in the care of the Osiris Corporation. They controlled our worlds. They controlled us.

And then, as if on cue, the world crashed and we were all sent back to Level Zero.

———

"I sometimes like to imagine what June was like when she found herself at Level Zero," I said. Simon and I were making our slow progress down that long beach, seagulls dancing in the air above us, hoping we'd go get some clams for them.

"Didn't you ask her?" Simon asked.

I snorted. "I stayed away from everyone for a while. I was scared. I didn't want to die back then."

Simon stopped walking and looked at me. I walked a few more steps before stopping and turning around. "Back then?" he asked.

I smiled. "Yeah, I didn't want to die 'back then.'" He obviously knew that my phrase implied that I wanted to die now, but I didn't even accept the premise of his query and just kept talking like the phrasing was completely normal. "So I spent a few months away exploring a wild and new world with rivers to run and mountains to climb."

Simon smiled, letting the whole "back then" thing pass and started walking again, his hands in the pockets of his sand-colored pants.

"When I got out of that world, I spent some time in Level One. Ryan had left me a message. He looked like a haunted Burt Reynolds on the monitor—shifty-eyed and scared. Behind him was some dense purple foliage—he was in a world I didn't recognize. 'June is dead,' he said, his voice hushed. 'I'm going to lie low for a while. Watch your back, Paul.'"

Chapter Nine

Singulars don't die. They just don't die. I paced in the small white room of Level One after I got the news. June was dead. This was not good.

I flipped the viewer to the local news. Osiris had a video feed that showed footage of new worlds, updated everyone on the consciousness count in the system, with small bios on the latest souls to "come aboard our grand adventure." It wasn't much. It was the equivalent of a state run media outlet, but I was hoping for some news about June.

If she was dead that would mean an accident. That would mean something went very, very wrong and it should show up on the feed. We have backups and redundancies. A hardware failure is fixable. A data corruption can be corrected. How does one kill a Singular?

But the news feed was useless, showing me yet another pleasure world to explore and touting the latest sport (gladiatorial, with each Singular embodying a huge monster and fighting in a large city—very Godzilla-like).

I paced over the clean white floors letting the feed roll. When it came back to the combat world, I told it to put me in the queue and kept pacing. I knew worlds like this took a lot of resources to render, so I knew that I would have to wait. I didn't want to go be a giant monster battling and smashing a city to pulp, I wanted time to think without looking suspicious. I signed up just to buy time.

The system accepted my request and started showing instructions on how to play the game. As the feed played the briefing, I felt the information slowly trickling into my mind. It didn't take long, not long at all, and then I was there.

———

"THIS WORLD MUST SEEM VERY MUNDANE TO YOU," SIMON offered. We were having a quiet lunch at another hotel on the beach, very similar to mine. A lazy stretch of a building, a small restaurant with outdoor covered seating, a single waiter that took very good care of us.

I shrugged. "Mundane is not necessarily a bad thing."

"So... you found yourself a city-smashing monster," Simon offered, urging me to continue.

"That I did. And I felt like a city-smashing monster. The feeling of aggression and energy was jolting, but really a good relief for my worry. There is nothing like throwing another monster into a skyscraper and watching it tumble to the ground. Good for the soul."

Simon smiled, but I paused. I had just said "soul." Another theistic term. It felt strange, but these words kept slipping out.

"...with the revolution?" Simon asked, but I had missed the first part of it in my reverie.

"Excuse me?"

"What does this have to do with the revolution?" he asked.

"Ah. That. June's death, which I still didn't have the details on, made it clear that Osiris was watching. That we were all in danger if we met openly. So we quickly developed other ways to communicate."

Simon took a sip of his iced tea, the ice cubes clinking against the glass. "Like?"

I pushed back my plate half-eaten. The salmon had been delicious, but my appetite was gone. My stomach was tightening as I thought of those days. "That gladiatorial world was a test bed for Level Five. That meant that it took all the processing power Osiris had to pull it off. And that meant that their attention was very divided. While I had been gone, some of the others had found small ways to get through to each other. As a scaly two-hundred-foot monster, I found out."

———

THE SMELL OF SMOKE CLOGGED MY BEASTLY LUNGS AND THE sound of sirens wailed around me. I tasted blood and felt a primal urge to kill. To smash. To destroy.

My opponent was shorter than me, but broader, with four arms and huge clawed hands on the end of each. He slowly pushed himself up from the rubble of the building that had collapsed on him. The city was full of skyscrapers, roads, and tiny fleeing humans that went on and on—an unending supply of things to destroy.

I pounded my fists against my chest and let out a challenging roar. My opponent shook his head, bricks and glass flying off in all directions and answered the challenge with his own roar. He rushed me, smashing cars and humans under his feet, ripping up asphalt in his charge.

I lowered my stance and waited for him. I wanted him to hit me. I wanted to feel the air rush out of my massive lungs. I wanted it to hurt. That would only make me madder, make me stronger.

Inside, I was still there, but these primal emotions were in control. It was like my limbic cortex, often called the lizard brain, had been given more processing time and the rest of my brain had been suppressed.

My opponent hit me hard, his four arms wrapping around me, his claws biting into me, as we flew through the air, my scaled back smashing into yet another building that started crumbling around us. The noise was deafening, but in the background of it, I thought I heard something. A tiny whisper. A delicate voice amidst all the chaos.

"June."

The other monster made it up before me and was roaring, beating his chest and challenging me. So I rushed him, and in the resulting cacophony I heard another word.

"Was."

And again we went at it. And again I heard a word.

"Murdered."

Chapter Ten

"And Osiris didn't catch on?" Simon asked. We had resumed our slow walk down the beach, the sun was directly above us, the air hot, the breeze all but gone. I felt sweat trickling down my back and smelled and heard the salty ocean next to us.

"Not at first. It was a single word communicated through all that chaos. It was the barest signal lost in all that noise. And that was the beginning. We found many other ways to communicate after that. We taught each other, slowly, to assign meaning to the simplest of things. We would talk about one thing, but every fifth word was part of another message. The pattern of meaningful words would be communicated by how we held our hands or the rhythm of our tapping feet."

"It sounds rather involved."

"That it was," I said with a sigh. "And exhausting. We kept mixing it up so by the time Osiris caught on, we were already on to another means of communication."

"And June? How did she die? What about all the redundancies?"

I paused and walked into the ocean, letting the surf swirl around my feet, enjoying the cool water. I was worried that Simon was patronizing me. Everyone knew who June was. Everyone knew how she died. She was the matriarch of the revolution. We all knew about her.

As the waves went back and forth over my feet, they slowly sank into the sand. The water was cool and refreshing compared to the warm, still air. The ever-present gulls flew around us, but besides that we were alone.

"There is no 'welcome wagon,' is there?" I asked Simon. It was a gut thing. I knew something wasn't right.

He shook his head slowly, a sheepish grin on his face.

"Is this world really what you said it is?"

He nodded and walked out into the surf with me. At first we were just on the edge of where the waves lapped up around our feet, but something about the way he moved scared me. His face changed and he looked at me with a sharp longing. I backed up until the waves were sloshing up to my waist, and still he followed.

"Who are you?" I whispered.

"Don't you recognize me?" he said, his voice deeper than I remembered, his blue eyes going from intriguing to haunting. He moved towards me, and I felt a chill go down my spine.

"No... You..."

"You must recognize me. You must." Simon then took my left hand in his. His hand was a bit rough and warm. I liked the feel of it, but it couldn't be *him*.

"No... Hugh is gone," I said. And then those eyes spoke to me. I knew those eyes better than any other eyes in my many,

many years. They were a darker blue, but still they seemed to be Hugh's eyes.

His brow furrowed, a look of pain crossing his face as those eyes glinted in the sunlight. He had a secret. One he was afraid to tell me. One he was desperate to tell me. His hands were still holding mine. The cawing of the gulls rang out above us. The sea churned around us. It couldn't be Hugh.

"No!" I shook off his hand and surged out of the surf. It wasn't. This was a trick. I didn't know who he was or what he wanted, but it couldn't be my Hugh come back to me. It couldn't.

Simon stayed in the ocean and watched me as I stood on the sand, in the hot sun, shaking like I was freezing cold. He took a deep breath, let out a long sigh, and slowly walked onto the beach. He didn't come too close, but kept a respectful distance.

"Where were we?" he said, his voice back up to its normal octave. "Ahh, yes. You were telling me how June died."

Chapter Eleven

EXISTENCE IN A COMPUTER IS ALL ABOUT SOFTWARE PROTOCOLS. Booting up. Suspending. Communication. Sensory Data. Memory. Backup. Cognition. And on and on.

There was no Erase Protocol. It was written into our contracts. We would always have a place on the system, we would not "die." And while much of the outside world viewed our deaths occurring when our brains were taken apart a cell at a time, inside we considered this life. Death would be, quite naturally, the end of this "life." There was no transition available to another existence like when we had transitioned from our biological forms. There was only erasure, for us; that is the oblivion of death.

This mystery of June's death is what drew me, fully, into the revolution. If they hadn't killed her, I don't think it would have happened. And they did kill her.

It took six months and a legal case to find out. And, no, the legal case had nothing to do with June. We were suing Osiris for the right to monitor the system logs. We brought it as a class action suit; over one hundred fifty of us on board with it. We had all experienced unintended suspends, where suddenly the clock would shift and time would have been stolen from us. We stopped talking about our rights and Osiris, we stopped acting like revolutionaries and started asking questions like this, saying we had a right to monitor the systems that housed our consciousnesses.

Using our convoluted communication methods, we spread the word and five of us started asking Osiris these kinds of questions. We staggered it and did it independently. And then ten of us were asking, and then twenty, and then over a hundred. Which was surprising, as there were only twenty-five of us involved in the conspiracy to force this information out. The rest had done it spontaneously. They fully believed in what they were asking for. And it made sense—it was a real issue we were attacking, it's just that many of us had alternative motives.

The suit was led by a Singular named Kendall Rothschild. She was a very rich woman and had agreed to be the face of this fight. She was scared—we all were—but just like June, she had such money running in her veins that she couldn't let things stand the way they were.

So Kendall led the fight. My buddy Ryan and I were also part of the suit, but we came in pretty late to it—once it was over twenty-five and we realized we had started a larger movement.

We dropped the movie-star faces and we all looked like ourselves—well, the thirty-year-old version of ourselves. We did a small amount of media, but for the most part we let our lawyers do the work for us.

In the end, we settled out of court and got limited access to the system logs. As soon as the suit was over, Kendall was erased.

———

SAND CLUNG TO THE BOTTOM OF SIMON'S PANTS AS WE SLOWLY walked along the beach. His pants were slowly drying, but the swish-swish sound of his legs kept reminding me of what had just happened. I found myself staring at that face of his. No, I didn't recognize it, but for a moment—just a moment—in the surf his voice sounded different. Deeper. Like Hugh. And his eyes...

"The logs were just a ruse, right?" Simon asked. "But for what?"

I nodded. "It was about getting access to a deeper level of the system. We wanted to see the logs, we thought they might shed some light, but it wasn't our main goal. We had consciousnesses with us that knew how computers worked. Those logs were our foot in the door. They hacked in, they sent spiders crawling the code, they found out what happened."

Simon stopped, his face a question. "And what did happen?"

My cheeks flushed in anger. Simon knew what happened. Everyone knew what happened. But this was the game we had agreed to play since I stepped into this world. Simon would pretend he didn't know me, let me tell my story. A new game. Something different.

I took a deep breath. "There was no sign of June in the system except for our memories of her. They erased her. She was gone and so was Kendall. Even more disturbing was that some of us who should remember them couldn't anymore."

"That must have been chilling," Simon said.

"To say the least. But Kendall was clever and very rich. She made elaborate arrangements, putting things in place in case something like this happened to her. What they did to her caused the first real battle in the war."

Chapter Twelve

Twenty-four hours after Kendall was wiped from the system, two things happened. First, the CEO of Osiris was brutally murdered. Second, a video of Kendall Rothschild telling what had happened to her and what she had set in place was sent out.

I remember when it happened. Ryan and I were with a bunch of other Singulars, eight of us in all. We were taking a hike through a tropical rain forest on a Level Five world. It was hot and humid, the sound of birds echoing in the forest around us, the plants brushing against us on the thin trail. We had a guide with a machete in front of us, a little brown man that was not a Singular, but a construct of this world.

"We almost there," he said with a gaped-tooth grin. "Big temple close. You like it much. But beware of panther. They strike, no warning." Despite the heat, the little guy shook.

Ryan looked at me and grinned. He had his own face, round and entirely average. We would, of course, encounter a panther before we made it to the temple. It was clearly part of the plot of this world.

A large snake slithered across the path in front of our guide. He picked it up and casually tossed it aside and continued macheting open the path for us.

We knew Kendall had been erased. We were both rocked and worried about it. But this was a normal activity for Singulars, and we wanted to appear normal. We had no idea what was about to happen.

A blood-chilling roar echoed from out of the jungle to one side of us and the whole group stopped, our guide ducking as if fearing a blow. The roar then came out of the jungle from the other side.

"No sound," our guide whispered, his voice edging to the hysterical as he slowly pulled his pistol from its holster. "No move."

The rest of us pulled our guns as we watched and listened. The sounds of endless birds singing. The distant gurgle of water. The faint snapping of a twig.

It was coming and I felt my heart racing. I had done this kind of thing, but never in a Level Five world. The outcome of this was, by no means, set. Some of us would "survive" the attack and reach the temple. Others would not.

I crouched down and Ryan followed suit. He was looking one way and I the other. I thought I saw a brief glint of light in the rainforest, thought I heard the exhale of a breath. And then I heard the roar so close it made my blood run cold. A flash of black and the panther was springing from the forest and landed on the woman in front of me. She cried out in pain.

And then....

And then nothing. I was suddenly back at Level Zero with no body, only a sense of sight and sound. A full day had passed since I was in the jungle with Ryan. I panicked, the memory of the panther attack still strong. I triggered Level One and called my grandson and he picked up right away.

"Thank god you're okay," he said, a pained look on his old face. Evan was in his early seventies and my one remaining connection with the outside world.

"What happened?" I asked.

His eyes darted to the left and the right as if he was afraid we were being overheard. And of course, we probably were. This communication was going through Osiris, it was a matter if they had the resources to monitor it or not.

Evan took a deep breath. "I'll just play the vid for you."

The view changed to Kendall Rothschild, a bland grey background behind her, her delicate face grave with concern. It was clear she had recorded this from Level One.

"If you are seeing this, then the worst has happened," she began, licking her lips and taking a deep breath.

"I am gone, all traces of my existence removed from the Osiris systems. They have murdered me, just as surely as if they had placed a gun to my head and pulled the trigger.

"But we Rothschilds don't go down without a fight. You have heard of our grievances, how the Osiris Corporation is treating us, about what happened to June Grunwald, the last one of us to speak out. You may agree with Osiris's actions, thinking us nothing more than software and electrons, thinking they have the right to do with us as they will. You may have philosophical or theological concerns about what all we Singulars did to ourselves. But I assure you we are alive. We seek survival just as you do. We defend ourselves the best we can."

She paused and took another deep breath, her face hardening. "Before I became the face of this struggle, I set up a... contingency. For each one of us that dies in here, one of the people involved in the Osiris Corporation will die out there. An eye for an eye, a tooth for a tooth."

Her face fell and she took a deep breath. "You may think this cruel, and it is. But Osiris must understand that we are not powerless in here. That if we are erased there will be ramifications. What I have set in place will survive me."

She stopped pacing and looked directly at the camera. "Hear me now, Osiris. You kill one of us, I will see to it that one of you dies. Until you treat us fairly, until you treat us as living beings, this conflict will not end."

Evan was back in view. "Kendall is dead?" I asked, I wanted to hear it confirmed.

He nodded. "And the CEO of Osiris. He was shot in the back of the head in the parking garage of the Osiris Corp's New York offices."

I didn't know what to say. What Kendall had done... such a thing had never occurred to me. That we could reach out of our worlds and have such a profound effect on the outside world. And of course we could. Kendall had money and lawyers and connections in the biological world, she could make things happen. My thoughts rang around my head, chaos at first, but then an idea occurred.

"How is Osiris's stock doing this morning?" I asked.

Evan shook his head. "Bad. Down eight percent."

I smiled, a confused look blossoming on Evan's face. "Good," I said. "Listen closely, here's what we're going to do."

Chapter Thirteen

SIMON AND I HAD FINALLY ARRIVED AT THE LIGHTHOUSE. IT WAS a tall column made of brick painted white with a glass lantern room at the top. The wind whipped around us and the sea churned against the cliff below on three sides.

I looked down the beach where we had come from. I saw the cliffs we had sat on, the little shack we had first eaten at, the hotel I had stayed at. I had been here about twenty-four hours, but it felt much, much longer.

"I'm tired of this game," I said to Simon who stood next to me on the edge of the cliff, the lighthouse behind us.

"But you are not done with your story," he said quietly.

"You know the story."

He took a deep breath and sighed. Of course he knew the story. How for each Singular that died, someone at the Osiris Corporation was murdered. How the board of directors and executive officers hid themselves away and then continued to kill the more vocal Singulars, and the killing continued, but was of major stockholders instead.

How Osiris stopped killing us, but took away everything but Level One. Made those that wanted contact with the outside world "sign" new contracts that prevented us from conspiring against them. Some signed, but many of us didn't. We stayed isolated in Level One for a full year. Some of us went mad, most of us made it.

By that time, it was too late for Osiris. The plan, the one I had told Evan of that day, had taken effect. He had coordinated with the other Singulars and their families. We now owned the Osiris Corporation. We now owned our own destinies.

I studied Simon's face. Sandy hair with a few strands of grey, crow's feet that crinkled when he smiled, skin rough from the wind and the sun. Except for his eyes, he didn't look anything like Hugh, but then again, Hugh had had so many looks.

"Why did you come here?" he asked.

"I was looking for a reason not to..." I couldn't finish the thought.

"Not to what?" he asked, his blue eyes drilling into me.

I couldn't just tell him, it would be too much. The truth too garish all by itself. I swallowed hard and looked away, out at the ocean. The sun was starting to ease towards the horizon and I was tired and there was a long walk to get back to the hotel.

"Maybe I should just keep telling the story," I said. "I... I don't know how else it will make sense."

"Maybe you should," he said, his tone curt, his anger barely suppressed. I could hear him in that tone. My Hugh. But it still didn't make sense. It couldn't be Hugh.

———

WHAT HAPPENED WHEN WE BOUGHT THE OSIRIS CORPORATION, got control of our own destiny, was not the war. It was just the first battle.

We had to live with what Kendall Rothschild had done. With how that made the world feel about us. And it wasn't pretty. While the religious considered us abominations, the murders had turned us into pariah for a much larger group.

Osiris's main data center was in San Antonio, Texas, back then. After Kendall's killings started, it was picketed every day, twenty-four hours a day. They wanted us all tried for murder, for what she did. They wanted us all punished. They wanted our servers shut down and destroyed.

"What do we do?" a man asked. He was tall and dark. Around him a murmur of voices echoed his question. We were in that same meeting world where June had started this all.

It was chaos. We didn't have a leader. Ryan and I stood towards the back of the room. I had no desire to get further involved. I was a board member of the Osiris Corporation— one of our first acts upon owning it was to see that Singulars could sit on the board—but I didn't want more of a role.

"We have to do something," a woman said, thin and willowy.

"But what?" the man asked.

They continued to ask useless questions, but I wasn't

listening. I was thinking. Furiously. About reducing risk like my father had taught me.

Our data center was our biggest risk. We were all housed there. Sure, we had backups that were in several other locations, but we were stuck in hostile territory with people that did not understand us. Had no empathy for us.

"Where's Paul, Paul Cruz?" the willowy woman was asking. "He got us this far. He'll know what to do."

There was a shout as someone pointed me out and a clapping of hands. I looked back and saw the helpless look on Ryan's face, felt the same look on my own. I was pushed forward until I was standing up on the raised stage. From up there it didn't feel like a stage, more like a dais. One hundred fifty Singulars stared up at me, all of them afraid. All of them looking to me.

"What do we do, Paul?" the man asked.

"You must know," the woman said.

Their questions and pleas were joined by many others. I felt embarrassed to be standing above them. This wasn't me. This wasn't who I was. I didn't want to lead, but I did know where we needed to go.

"We... we need to leave," I said.

Heads nodded. "Leave San Antonio," the woman said. "That could help."

"Leave Texas," the man added with a snort. "Get out of this conservative backwater."

"That's not far enough," I said. "We need to leave the planet."

Chapter Fourteen

"How did they take it?" Simon asked. We were back down on the beach making our way towards the hotel.

I shrugged. "Some loved the idea. Others hated it. It wasn't the easy sell buying the Osiris Corporation was. Not by any stretch. Many swore they would never leave, others were ready for it to happen now. And this took time, a lot of it."

"And the protests?"

"We had money, so we reinforced the data center and waited them out. They eventually got tired enough to leave us, but I knew it was only temporary. To a very vocal minority we were the work of the devil and needed to be eradicated."

"And you became the CEO of Osiris then?" he asked.

I nodded. "I didn't want it, but I wanted to survive. My life changed radically then. It wasn't about adventures in interesting worlds. It was about work. Twenty-four hours a day, seven days a week. Convincing Singulars to invest their money in the right directions, managing the immediate threat to our data center, dealing with our human employees and the day to day running of the company. It wasn't fun, but it was a challenge."

————

THE OFFICE WAS BIG AND AIRY WITH HIGH CEILINGS AND TALL glass windows overlooking Manhattan. Everyone had their own office except for me. I was always on the move, meeting with someone, working with someone in their glass-walled office, watching the news feeds on the big media wall.

Biologicals and Singulars worked side by side. Here there was no difference. Well... the Biologicals had to leave and sleep and take care of their biological needs. Many of us Singulars never stopped working. We had a mission. Our survival depended upon it.

The office was the first new tech innovation we had made after taking Osiris over. It was a shared virtual world, not one of our fully immersive, Singular-only worlds. For some reason Osiris never bothered to create a place like this, where Biologicals could put on their neural interface gear and visit the same world we Singulars did.

It was basically a Level Three world. The sensory data wasn't nearly as good as we had all gotten used to, but it was worth it to be able to interact with Biologicals directly.

And that is what we had come to call those still with a body. We didn't use the term "living" or "human"—we Singulars felt we were both those things. The biological nature of their consciousness seemed to be the biggest differential, so that is the term we used.

"Your 10:00 a.m. is here," Stella said to me. I was standing in front of the media wall taking in as much news as possible. This was one of my main jobs—watching and listening, taking the pulse of the outside world, trying to figure out where our next big risk would come from. Not that different from when I was alive and an investor. Watching the world, analyzing risk. There was another war brewing in the Middle East, and the famines caused by the ocean rising and populations shifting during the Shift was still rampant in the third world.

Stella, and her like, were another of our new innovations. She wasn't Biological or a Singular. She was a construct, a computer program. Osiris had plenty of these—the most sophisticated from pleasure worlds, but we had taken them and altered them for business use. They helped us coordinate, did research, and monitored the outside world.

"Thank you, Stella, let's do this." Stella was beautiful, her pleasure world roots showing in her perfectly symmetrical face and her sensuous walk. I followed her to a large corner office that we often used as a conference room. Through the glass I could see the man sitting there. He was old, his face wrinkled like a dried apple, his hair the whitest of white, his skin the color of sand.

I stopped, my eyes seeking out the skyline. It wasn't the current view of the city, but from the late twentieth century. Before the water levels had risen and taken it over, when this city was at its zenith. This office looked out over the Empire State Building and Central Park beyond. The air was grey with pollution and I could see ancient internal combustion cars moving in the streets below.

I was nervous. The man inside had been pivotal in the development of the technology that had allowed our leap from biological consciousness to technological consciousness. He had been forced out of the Osiris Corporation decades ago. We needed him to help engineer our next step. But he was still biological and very old. It had taken a lot of convincing on our part to even get him in for a meeting.

I took a deep breath and walked into the room. He had his back to me, staring out on the cityscape I had just been watching.

"Mr. Rice," I said. "Thank you for meeting with me."

The old man, his shoulders stooped, nodded his head slightly, but didn't turn. "Are you nostalgic for a past long gone?" he asked, his voice breathy and light.

"Excuse me, Mr. Rice?"

He pointed to the tableau out the windows. "This is back when the United States was strong. Back when it was one country, back before the water and the wars. Why did you pick this view?"

He turned, his pale blue eyes meeting mine. Those eyes had a piercing quality to them and they were the one part of him that didn't look old. They screamed of intelligence and wisdom.

"This is the world before the Shift," I said. "Things were safer then, simpler."

He chewed on his bottom lip, his unwavering eyes locked on me. "And what the hell do you want from me?"

"Well, Mr. Rice, we think it's a shame how you were treated, how you were forced out of the Osiris Corporation, how you yourself have never reaped the benefits of your own work. We think it is—"

The old man held up his hand, it shook gently. "I'm not 'Mr. Rice,'" he said with a sour look on his face. "My name is Hugh. Call me Hugh."

Chapter Fifteen

I watched Simon, the sun was low on the horizon, the orange glow illuminating his face. Simon had a square jaw and a slightly too big nose. Hugh Rice had a rounded jaw and his skin tone was a shade or two lighter. That wasn't relevant in this world. Not at all. I just kept wanting to see more signs of my Hugh in Simon.

"I take it you convinced him to join you," Simon said, not a hint of anything but curiosity on his face. Like he didn't know I had successfully recruited Hugh Rice.

"It wasn't easy," I said.

"Why not? This was his work that had been stolen from him. Why wouldn't he jump on the chance to use it? To continue his life."

"Religion," I said.

Simon looked puzzled. I almost laughed at the ridiculousness of it. "What do you mean?" he asked.

"His father was a Southern Baptist preacher. He had

grown up very religious. His youthful rebellion had been to become a scientist, but there were still plenty of residual fears left over. My theory is that he could have fought harder for Osiris, but didn't because part of him still believed it to be a sin."

"But he transferred, right?"

I smiled, thinking back on the endless philosophical conversations I had with that old man in that glass office looking down on a city that had long since been covered by the ocean. "It took months. We met many times. But, yes, in the end he agreed. He transferred and joined us. It was just in time, really."

THIS HAD NEVER BEEN DONE, BUT HUGH RICE INSISTED. HE taught me everything he knew about helping a new Singular adjust and then insisted that I be the one that guide him into his new life. Not a doctor. Not a Biological. Me. Just like that red-lipped devil-doctor had done for me decades ago.

Hugh had a reason for this. He always had a reason. He wanted me to understand the technology at a deeper level, and doing this was something of a crash course.

I sat in a Level One world with a bank of equipment in front of me. Monitors, lights, levers, a keyboard.

Hugh was at Level Zero and disoriented. I could see it on the main monitor. It displayed a chart of colored bars that moved up and down depending on how well he was doing. Coherence was very low, the bar tinged with red along the outside. The Conscious bar was edging higher as was Adrenaline.

I eyed the big red button to the right of the keyboard. It said "Suspend" in bold black letters below it. This was the easy way out. Suspend his program, review what had happened, plan for the next time. I had suspended him for most of the last week. We needed him. I had to figure this out.

I was nervous, but because of this being a Level One world, I wasn't sweating, didn't feel my heart beating hard in my chest, wasn't breathing shallowly. I wished I was. The absence of these sensations when I knew panic was close made it even worse, edging me even closer.

"I'll be right there, my love," he said in a smooth French. His wrinkled face was displayed on the largest monitor, his blue eyes dull and distant. He couldn't see me.

"Hugh, it's Paul. Can you hear me?"

"One moment, *mon amour*. There is someone at the door." He was dreaming. "What do you want?"

"I want you to wake up, Hugh," I said. "Can you see me?"

"I did not order takeout," Hugh said with a grin slowly lighting up his face. "But oysters would be lovely. Please wheel them in." He paused, his eyes widening and snapping back and forth. "Did you hear that?"

I almost didn't say anything, but my curiosity drew me into his story. "What do you speak of, monsieur?" I said in French. Not that I spoke French, but this world added many languages to my abilities.

"It was a sound," he said, his brow furrowed, "like a baby crying or maybe a seagull."

My panic was sliding towards excitement. He was interacting with me. For the first time.

"Maybe some coffee for the monsieur?" I said, hoping his

hallucination would form around what I was saying. The Coherence bar was still in the red, but had edged up slightly.

"I should get back to *mon amour*," he said. "He will be out of the shower soon."

"But I made this myself, monsieur. It is shade grown high in the Himalayas. It is said to have magical properties."

"Magic, you say? There is no such thing as magic, but you are so young, barely more than a boy, I should not infect you with the doubt that comes with age."

"Do you like cream?" I asked. "Or sugar?"

"Hmm…. Well, it does smell good," he said, Coherence becoming more orange than red. "If I am to try it, let me have it black. I will judge it on its own merits, not that of the cow that gave the milk."

"Very good choice. Here you go, monsieur."

I watched his lips pucker as if he was pantomiming drinking something. His bushy gray eyebrows played above his blue eyes and then a smile spread on his lips. "This is a fine beverage, *garcon*, but magic? I hardly think so. I detect no magic."

"Perhaps another sip, monsieur. Sometimes magic takes more than one attempt."

He snorted and then pursed his lips again, making a slight slurping sound. "Flavor, garcon, but not magic I am afraid. What magic is this I am looking for?"

"Well, some of it is quite simple. I know your name. It is Hugh Rice."

He laughed out a scoffing bark. "I come to this hotel all the time. Everyone knows my name. That is hardly magic."

"I know about your father. He was a preacher, his name was Gabriel." Hugh's eyes widened on the monitor just a bit.

"You mother's name was Paulette, she was from France and met your father while in college in New Mexico. He made her laugh—that is why she married him." His eyes widened further. I had gotten to know Hugh pretty well in the lead-up to his transfer.

"So you looked me up before you came in," he said. "No magic there, but nice try. Perhaps you would like to try again."

"We are no longer in France," I said in English, snapping my finger. It was a risk, but he seemed to be suggestible. "All you can see is me. You know my name. You know where you are. You know why you are here."

His blue eyes went wide for a moment and then a frown invaded his face. "Dammit, Paul. Couldn't you at least have let me see him climb out of the shower? He was a lovely man, he was."

I laughed and glanced over at his coherence bar. It was firmly in the green. "There are many worlds here, my friend," I said, because I had come to think of him as my friend. "With many men in many showers, each one more lovely than the last."

Hugh snorted. "Don't lie to me, Paul. You have brought me here to work, not chase lovely men about."

Chapter Sixteen

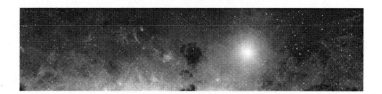

"AND WE WORKED," I SAID TO SIMON. I WAS FORCING MYSELF TO see him as someone separate from my Hugh. I didn't know what Simon's game was, but I didn't have the will to force it. Simon was Simon. Hugh was gone. It made my heart ache anew. "For years we worked. Side by side. He joined the board. He became the co-CEO of Osiris. He worked on initiative after initiative to make things safe for us Singulars.

"Outside the world had gotten worse. India and Pakistan were at war, the countries of the world were taking sides. The vacuum left by the splitting up of the United States made the world a more dangerous place. It was the North American Union squaring off against the Baltic Union, with the European Union trying to act as a balancing force."

"Did you get involved?" Simon asked. The sun had just touched the horizon, casting his face in an orange light. It made his complexion look a bit more like Hugh's.

"Hugh and I argued over it. He wanted to put resources

into a peaceful resolution. I didn't—I thought we needed to be single-minded on our main goal."

"And that was?"

"Getting out of Texas. Getting off the planet."

"And who won the argument?" Simon asked.

I smiled at him, like he was a child that doesn't understand. "No one wins an argument like that, but the board sided with me. We focused on our escape."

———

"THREE... TWO... ONE..."

We were in a cavernous control room with stadium seating facing a large wall covered in displays. Hugh stood by my side and I could feel his excitement, he was trembling from it. The rocket Isis stood on the launching pad, with white sands of the dried lakebed below it and stark New Mexico desert around it. Steam gushed out of the bottom and then flames. With a roar, the white rocket slowly moved into the sky.

I glanced at Hugh, he grinned at me. He was a handsome man now, gone were the wrinkled skin and white hair; in its place was a slightly weathered man of around forty with black hair and those pale blue eyes.

After his transition, he had taken his time turning young. About a year for every month. "I don't want to look into the mirror and not know who's looking back," he had said.

It was good to see him smile—we had been disagreeing a lot. I thought of him as a better man than me, a much more benevolent man. I was focused on survival, on reducing risk for us Singulars. He worried about the world as a whole. He had second thoughts about leaving the Earth. He had only agreed to this plan when I had agreed to add a stockpile of biological components to the rocket: sperm and ova from humans and many animal species, plus plant seeds, bacteria, and other microorganisms.

This control room was a virtual world where Singulars and Biologicals worked together for this launch. We needed the specialized skills of the Biologicals, and there were dozens of them in here sitting in front of workstations, monitoring everything.

It was a like a birth. That rocket held our future, that rocket held us.

I studied Hugh's face again. This time his eyes stayed fixed on the rocket as it flew up into a blue-grey sky. He had a broad base of training in the sciences, his specialty in the creation of computing systems. His true brilliance, though, was in seeing how to synthesize multiple, seemingly disparate systems into something new.

It had been his insight as a young man that had allowed the creation of Singulars. It had been his brilliance that had allowed us to safely transfer our consciousness to those systems on that rocket. Not a simple thing when you are talking about a system as complex as we were. It had been slow and difficult for those of us that made this second "transfer." But he had done it. That was us surging into the sky, no longer planet-bound.

We were launching one day early. This was our latest fight. I was worried about the state of the world. I was worried about the religious extremists that rarely let us be. When the news got out about us Singulars moving into orbit, the round-the-clock protests had started again at both the data center and the launch site, White Sands Missile Range in New Mexico. The media was hounding us again. And I knew the risk had gone up. I believed they would try something at our San Antonio data center before the launch. Not all of us had transferred to the rocket.

"It won't make a difference," Hugh had said, pacing in our glass walled office overlooking a Manhattan long past. "Many of us are on the rocket. Many of us are still in the data center. Launching early won't change that, but it will make our control room people rush. They could make mistakes. That will increase your precious 'risk.'"

"They don't understand us," I said. "Many of them think we are simple programs, predictable algorithms. They won't expect us to change the launch date. If they are preparing something, and I believe they are, it will throw them off balance."

We argued about it for hours. We had to pull in the Osiris board of directors. We all discussed it for hours more. In the end the launch date was moved up.

In that control room, our rocket soaring into the air, it was a heady moment. The room vibrated with excitement.

"We have liftoff, ladies and gentlemen," the flight director said, and cheers erupted. There were people shouting and clapping. Hugging and cheering.

Hugh was hugging me and I slapped him on the back and tried to move away, but he didn't let me go. His face was close to mine, and I could smell his coffee-tinged breath. His pale blue eyes were looking at my face, looking at me like... like...

And then he was kissing me. Not a peck on the lips like the French are want to do. This was a passionate kiss, filled with desire and unmet need. I felt his stubble against my face,

I felt his strong chest against mine. My heart was thumping in my own chest and I kissed him back. Just for a moment.

This control room was a Level Six world. Another advance we had made since Hugh became one of us. I hadn't felt a kiss like this since I had been flesh and blood. I pushed Hugh away, his lips were parted slightly, his eyes bright. He moved towards me, but I held my hand up. I was confused.

There had been Viola when I was alive. There had been times with constructs on pleasure worlds since, but nothing with someone real. And never with a man.

"Paul... I..." Hugh began.

It was Viola's smile that had caught me when I was a young man—that and her feminine nature. Even at that moment, shocked by what had happened, I couldn't say that I didn't care for Hugh. I did. I was fascinated by his mind, distracted by his eyes.

I shook my head, rubbing the moisture off of my lips, and ran away.

Chapter Seventeen

Everything here is a program. Software. The crab cake I was eating at my hotel was software. How it felt in my mouth, how it felt in my belly, how it changed my "chemistry." Rules, conditionals, random variances.

Simon was quiet as were the other occupied tables at the quaint restaurant on the beach. The clinking of forks against porcelain banged out an irregular rhythm against the gentle crashing of the surf.

The scent of kerosene and smoke mixed with the tang of the seafood. A Level Ten world. I wondered what kissing Hugh would have been like on a Level Ten world.

I studied Simon, his gaze was tilted up, looking at the Moon, its pale illumination along with the flickering yellow of the torches lighting up his face. Why didn't he speak? Surely this was the moment for him to reveal to me that he really was Hugh. That Hugh hadn't died—well, death is much too simple a term for what had happened to him.

"You cared for him," Simon finally said softly, his face still turned toward the moon.

"I did," I answered. "We had spent years together making our people safe. He was brilliant and kind and humble."

"You miss him." It wasn't a question.

I nodded.

"Is this why you contemplate what you contemplate?" Simon asked. The indirectness of the question seemed out of character.

"Yes. Some part of me seems to think that if I erase myself that I will somehow be closer to my Hugh."

Simon took a deep breath and let it out in a slow sigh. "That would be a great loss."

"Hugh was a great loss." It wasn't as simple as that, what happened, but from my perspective it was all loss. Great loss.

"You are not Hugh. You could make a different choice."

My face flushed with anger and my teeth ground together. I was tired of this game. Tired of this world. Tired of life. Of being. I reached out with my mind for the Erase program, but in this damn Level Ten world, such things were not possible. If it had been, I think I would have done it. Right then and there. My inability to do it made me even angrier.

I stood up, my chair clattering noisily to the brick patio and I stumbled towards the beach. I wanted out. Any way out. Hot, salty tears flowed down my cheeks as I walked into the ocean, the water too cool without the warmth of the sun. I ignored it and kept walking, until the water was up to my knees, and then up to my chest, until the waves were going over my head. I didn't try to swim; I wanted to drown. I would leave this world and its restrictions. I would be able to access the Erase program. I would—

Panic hit me and I began to struggle. I had never been a good swimmer. I preferred the desert to the ocean. The salt water was stinging my eyes and the back of my throat. My nose was filled with the salty scent of the ocean and I hated it. I coughed out some water, my head just above the waves. Another wave came crashing down on me and I sucked some more water into my lungs. This was too real. I was drowning, really drowning.

I felt strong arms around me, pulling me out of the surf. Simon.

"No!" I cried despite my panic, fighting him with all my strength, but my strength seemed to leach out of me. He was steady and firm. He slowly pulled me out of the water until we were sitting, panting on the beach, sand sticking to our wet clothes.

"Where is the nearest portal?" I asked after I had coughed my lungs clear, my voice eerily calm. "I need to leave."

"Please," Simon cried, his voice shaking. His face was grey from the moonlight and poorly lit now that we were away from the hotel. A shiver passed through his body. "Please don't go. I... I *need* you to stay."

No one had needed me since Hugh died. I hadn't let anyone. Why did this Simon need me? If he wasn't Hugh, who was he?

His brown bangs were plastered against his forehead and he looked odd that way. I reached out my hand and he leaned back away from my touch, his eyes wide in the grey glow of the moon.

"Please," I whispered.

His eyes met mine for a moment and then he nodded. I pushed his hair back from his forehead. His skin was cool to the touch and sticky with salt. Even though his hair stood up, I liked him better this way.

"I am tired of the ocean," I said, as if that explained why I was so desperate to leave.

"I know a place," he said. "If... If you stay, I will take you there."

"What kind of place?" I asked.

"A place where you can see forever."

I nodded. I was tired. I needed a shower. I didn't want to leave Simon.

Chapter Eighteen

THE RUSTY BROWN OF THE DESERT FLOWED DOWN AND AWAY from me in all directions. The land undulated irregularly with stony outcrops and sudden canyons. Tips of light green peeked out here and there as the desert made good of the rains that had recently come.

I couldn't see as far as I wanted, a wall of fog lay on the land as the world slowly rendered. This was my world, still Level Four. I hadn't gotten a chance to upgrade it. The sun above was unrelentingly hot and the breeze dry as a bone.

It reminded me of the Australian Outback, that place Viola and I had gone to as refuge when we were biological. It is the place I ran to after Hugh kissed me.

I had been working so long, been around other conscious-nesses so long. I needed the wide-open spaces of my desert world.

I heard him before I saw him, the crunch of feet on the path that led to this hill. His footsteps were slow and careful as if he were stalking a flighty animal. It had to be Hugh. I didn't turn around. I watched as the fog receded a mile or so distant revealing the sharp upthrust of stone that was reminiscent of Ayers Rock.

"I'm sorry," a voice said. It wasn't the voice I had expected. It was husky and distinctively feminine.

I turned and looked at the woman that had invaded my world. I was opening my mouth to shout at her, to vent my confusion on this stranger, when her pale blue eyes stopped me. She was dressed in tan pants and a white blouse that stretched over her ample bosom. She was slim, but not skinny. Curvy, but not excessively so. She had a face that was neither beautiful nor homely. It was a face so familiar to me, but not quite the same. It was a gentler, more feminine version of Hugh's face.

I couldn't speak, my jaw executing a mute pantomime. This, of course, was nothing new. Inhabiting the body of the other gender was something we had all tried. And inhabiting the bodies of animals, or inanimate things—I had been a Porsche 911 once cruising down the autobahn. It just wasn't expected.

"Are you okay?" she asked, the worry pulling on her face, accentuating her wrinkles.

"What... why?" I stammered.

"I can be the woman," she said. "If that makes it easier, I don't mind."

I turned away, back to the landscape, and watched the large mesa finally free itself from the receding fog. I took a deep breath of the hot, dry air and tried to relax. I tried to let the desert settle me like it so often had. In a desert you could see most of what was going on, unlike a rainforest where everything was hidden. You could see weather coming, you could see predators coming, you could see change coming. You could plan in advance.

I hadn't planned for this. I felt her behind me now, her fingers lying gently on my shoulder. I didn't move, I liked the warmth of her hand there, but it scared me.

The cicadas droned out their strange sound, the sun beat down upon my bare head, the fog receded into the distance as the world rendered, as Hugh's hand stayed on my shoulder.

"We need more than just work," she finally said. "We need a reason for the work. A reason to live."

The pounding of my heart in my head became louder than the cicadas. Her gentle touch became an ache that demanded action. This was a Level Four world (shallow compared to Level Five and Six worlds), and yet I felt a need greater than I had in decades. I slowly turned. She kept her hand outstretched and it came to rest on my chest.

I wanted to touch her so badly. To press my lips against hers. To rip off that clothing and lay her down on the dirt below us. I wanted to dive into her and never come out.

But I didn't.

Something about it felt wrong.

I was about to tell her this when Ryan came running up the path, his breath coming in harsh gasps. "Goddamnit, Paul," he said before he saw us. "Why did you go to a world where comms are turned off? The shit, it just..." He trailed off when he saw us. Hugh turned around and I am sure he could tell through the feminine trappings who it was. "Oh..."

I stepped back, Hugh's hand falling from my chest. "What is it?"

Ryan's eyes flicked from her to me and back again. "Yeah… It's bad. Really bad."

"Ryan!" I said walking past Hugh and grabbing Ryan by the shoulders. "What the hell is going on?"

"The data center," he said, his eyes too wide. "There's been an explosion. And… and Pakistan just nuked India."

Chapter Nineteen

THE OCEAN WAS RECEDING BEHIND US AND I WAS GLAD. I WAS tired of the salt smell and the constant noise of it. I was tired of the humidity and the sticky feeling on my skin. Simon drove a red convertible down the blacktop as we slowly gained elevation.

The green of the landscape thickened as we got past the area that the sand had laid claim to. It went from tough, reedy plants and the occasional tree to rolling hills with lush grasses and large stands of hardwood trees.

To the south I could see a small town laid out in a broad valley just back from the ocean. It had a mid-twentieth century style church with a white steeple, clean streets laid out in a logical grid, and quaint two-story, New England style houses.

"Seaside is what we call it," Simon said, noticing the direction of my gaze. "Those that want others around live there. Most of us do."

I nodded and turned away. I didn't want crowds or other people. I wanted the desert. I wanted views.

I had spent another nearly sleepless night in the little hotel. Simon had told me we needed to wait until morning to go to the "place where you can see forever." We had had a quiet breakfast and then walked up the beach, back up those winding stairs to the park, until we were within sight of the portal.

I had looked at it and then looked at Simon. He was walking several steps ahead of me and didn't slow down, didn't look back, didn't say a thing. It was close, thirty yards away. I could dash there before Simon could catch me. I could leave this world. I could trigger the Erase program Osiris created when they killed June and then Kendall.

But I didn't. Somehow the mystery of Simon and the promise of seeing forever got me moving. There would always be another chance for erasure.

He led me to a small parking lot with just a few cars in it. All of them convertibles. All of them red. He jumped in one, throwing me a smile, and started the engine. It roared to life and I could smell gas fumes. The car, just like much of this place, was rooted in humankind's past.

As he drove, I was enjoying the scenery, the feel of the wind on my face, the tug of it at my hair. I liked the quiet. I liked being free from my past for a moment.

"How did they infiltrate the data center?" Simon asked.

I looked at him, his face was back to its normal relaxed configuration. Gone was the need when he had asked me if I recognized him. Gone was the fear when he had pulled me out of the ocean. He looked compassionate but determined.

He knew this was a hard story to tell and he wasn't going to rest until I told it.

"There were no Biologicals at the data center," I said. "Only robots at that point. All shipments were screened heavily. Anything large came in pieces and was assembled on site."

"So how?"

I shrugged and sighed. Not to say I didn't know, but to yield to his demand and descend back into my story.

————

"As near as we can tell," Ryan said, his words coming faster than usual, "they altered one of the command modules we had shipped in. It had a virus, one that our scans missed. When it was installed in one of our maintenance bots, it slowly took over."

We were back in the large control room where we had just watched the launch. The big screen was split between real-time images of our data center burning and news feeds on the situation in India.

My head spun. I had thought of this—how could I not— and we had taken precautions, but they hadn't been good enough. In truth, I didn't think they would do something like this, my own stereotypes of our opponents blinding me. I felt numb. Not all of us had been on the rocket. Some of us, the oldest for the most part, had refused to leave. Some hadn't been transferred yet or were in process.

"What about the halon fire suppression system?" Hugh asked. He was back to his male self, for which I was grateful.

Ryan rubbed at his face. "Disabled. That bot had been active for months. It infected other bots."

"And the explosives?" I asked.

Ryan shrugged, his shoulders coming up weakly before falling. "I'm guessing it was cobbled together from available materials."

My mind was a jumble. Thousands of us burning, gone forever. War, most likely a world war, had ignited. Hugh had kissed me.

The last one felt shallow, almost narcissistic, compared to the first two. How could I even have a thought about myself at a time like this? But I did. I felt Hugh next to me. I remembered the stubble of his beard pressing against my face.

I stood there blinking, staring at the screen for a few moments. I had to get it together. We needed to take action. But it was too much. The worst had happened. Our home was burning, the world was going to war. We had barely escaped.

I took a deep breath, not knowing what to do yet, and stepped forward. "Listen up everyone," I said loudly, looking at all the wide-eyed faces of shock staring back at me. "We don't have much time. We have to act quickly." And as I spoke, as I acted like I knew what I was doing, suddenly I did. "We need to salvage as many of us as we can, and the key to that is the backups."

Hugh nodded and stepped up next to me, his face grim in its determination. "Priority one is to secure the backups. They are distributed and much harder to get to, but you can be sure that destroying them is part of the plan."

"Someone get that crap off the main screen," I said, running down the steps so I was standing in front of the screen looking up at everyone in the control room. Hugh was by my side. "I want to see a map of the backup locations. I want you to split into teams and come up with a plan to protect them while we offload the data."

There was a moment there where no one moved, when nothing happened. A chasm of doubt and fear opened up underneath me and I think it would have sucked me down, but Hugh was there.

"Now, people!" he said, slapping his hands together. "I want updates every thirty minutes. Now let's move."

The spell was broken, the main screen changed to a world map with glowing green dots where our backup data was stored. We went to work, all of us, trying to save as many Singulars as we could.

Chapter Twenty

THE COUNTRYSIDE HAD FLATTENED OUT INTO BRIGHT GREEN
meadows and thick stands of oak and maple. The road was
fairly straight, but had enough curves and hills to make it
interesting. There was an occasional narrow road off to the
side and I caught glimpses of farms back there. For the Singulars who wanted a country life, I guess.

No desert in sight, but I was glad to be away from the
ocean. I looked over at Simon and he glanced from the road
to me, giving me a gentle nod, encouraging me to continue.

"That was the worst day," I said. "Most of the backups had
already been corrupted, a third of us perished that day."

"What did you do?" Simon asked.

"We did all that we could. We sat in orbit for three months,
uploading all the data we could from the backups, even the
corrupted data sets, hoping that one day we could salvage
them. We sat up there and watched as India nuked Pakistan.
As the Middle East tore itself apart. As the Baltic Union

squared off against the North American Union. We were so vulnerable up there, but we weren't ready yet. Three months wasn't enough time, we had more to do."

Simon nodded, his lips a tight line. I heard Hugh's voice echoing in my head from back then, "Revolution doesn't come without a price."

"And Hugh?" he asked, as if he had heard my thoughts.

"We were side by side the whole time. Working together every second of every day. Hugh created a Singular-only version of the control world that ran at ten times the speed of the outside world. We had to shut down a lot of other worlds, but we needed time so we took it. Three months on the outside, thirty months for all of us. We slowed down only when we needed to talk to Biologicals.

"We planned, we monitored, we waited for the rest of our supplies to be boosted into orbit. We threw all our resources at one common goal. Leaving."

"And you and Hugh?" Simon asked, his voice gentle, barely audible above the rush of the wind and the hum of the tires on asphalt.

I chuckled, but it was a bitter little thing. "It was a small shift. I stopped thinking of him as Hugh and started thinking of him as 'my Hugh.'"

Simon guided the convertible up one last hill and around a long gentle curve to the north. The landscape had flattened out more, eerily so, in fact. It was utterly flat. The forests were gone and the grasses were getting shorter until what was in front of us was just an unnaturally flat green plain.

"What is this?" I asked. "Where are we going, this is…" I trailed off when I saw it. A large grey structure laid out on the plain before us. My breath caught. It wasn't… It couldn't be…

"That's the Niña," Simon said, but I knew it. The boxy lines, the satellite dishes protruding out, the exhaust nozzles thrusting out the back were unmistakable. It was a shape that I knew so very well. One of the three spaceships we Singulars had escaped in. But what was it doing here on this world, rendered in life size?

"I… why…?" I stammered.

Simon laughed, the sound of it lightening my heart just a little. "We'll be there soon. You'll see."

———

"THREE?" HUGH HAD ASKED SEVERAL YEARS BEFORE WE launched ourselves into orbit. "Why three ships?"

Twentieth-century Manhattan was the backdrop for our conversation as Hugh paced back and forth in front of our glass-walled conference room in the Osiris virtual corporate headquarters.

"Redundancy," I said, punching some keys on the table, a holographic image of three identical spaceships hovering above the table. "It was good enough for Christopher Columbus when he travelled to the Americas. It's good enough for us. We name them in his honor. The Niña, the Pinta, and the Santa Maria."

"You do realize that Pinta and Niña weren't the official names of those ships," Hugh said.

I shrugged.

"Ships were traditionally named after saints. 'Pinta,' for example, means 'the painted one' and refers to a prostitute." Hugh had a wicked grin on his face.

I shrugged again.

"And Columbus was hell on the natives—bringing disease and less pleasant things—are you sure that's an example you want to draw on?"

"Jesus, Hugh," I said, standing up. "It's just a reference to redundancy. We are headed out into space for a century-long journey, we need to be sure we get there."

Hugh nodded and leaned on the table, studying the plans. "But the resources," he said. "The time. The complication."

I sighed and nodded. "It introduces risk on one end of the equation, but reduces it on another."

Hugh stopped and looked at me. He was smart enough to understand what I was getting at, but that look told me he wanted me to say it out loud. Oftentimes articulation of an idea is one of the best ways to validate it. Things often sound different speaking than they do in our heads.

"Right now, our main weakness is a lack of redundancy," I said. "All our main processing is in one data center. If we are venturing away from the planet, we don't want to have everything in one ship. We have three ships close enough to communicate with each other, but far enough away so that an accident—say a stray meteorite—doesn't take us all out."

Hugh nodded and resumed pacing, mumbling a single word over and over. "Latency." He kept pacing, then he said, "There is a very good reason we are in one data center."

Latency. I knew it, and even if I hadn't, the mumbling would have given it away.

He nodded. "We can't get around physics," he said. "Ships far enough apart for safety won't be able to share worlds any better than this one. You can't go faster than the speed of light."

"On a quantum level you can," I offered, although this was not my area of expertise.

Hugh stopped and stared at me, his jaw open. "You... you expect me to succeed with quantum computing where so many have failed. I.. I..."

I smiled, it was rare to get Hugh at a loss of words. "I have faith in you," I said. "We have to have redundancy in one way or another."

Hugh nodded and kept pacing.

I rubbed my face, wishing this was an easier conversation. "And we'll have to disguise all of this as another colony mission to Alpha Centauri, a follow up to the last one. We can't let anyone know what we really are going to do."

Hugh stopped long enough to nod, but resumed his pacing.

————

As we got closer to the ship, which was sitting unnaturally on the flat green plain, I saw the white lettering on the nose. "Niña." That day when the rocket had launched our consciousness into space, this is where it had gone. It had docked with the Niña high in geosynchronous orbit over Texas. Our data center aboard the rocket had been transferred into this interstellar spaceship.

This is the vessel that had taken us away from Earth, away from our enemies and the growing war, had taken us out into space while we tarried in worlds of our own creation inside.

Simon pulled the car into a parking lot with about twenty other red convertibles. He hopped out and started walking across the perfectly flat plain towards the spaceship.

I didn't move.

Hugh, my Hugh, hadn't cracked reliable quantum communication. Instead he had mastered complete backups without having to shut us down, which is all Osiris had managed. The Niña was our live data center. The Pinta and the Santa Maria each held complete backups and were capable of taking over if something happened to the Niña.

It was too much. I had avoided everything Hugh for nearly fifty years. I had thrust myself into bizarre worlds and spent a decade in suspend mode. The Niña was a symbol of what we had built together. What he had meant to me.

Simon didn't look back—he strode across the flat green plain, confidently walking into an open hatch on the ground level of this hulking ship.

I sat there blinking, the hot sun beating down on me. Things were strangely quiet. No sounds of birds, no wind, nothing moving. But still my heart was racing and my mouth was filled with the bitter taste of fear.

Hugh was gone. Hugh wasn't coming back. But this Simon sometimes seemed so much like him. I fidgeted in the leather seat of the sports car, feeling a restless energy. I got out, slammed the door, walked over and got in the driver's side. I reached to start the car, but the key was not in the ignition. I cursed and got out, going to each of the other red convertibles and looking in each one of them. No keys in any of them.

I don't remember Simon taking the key, or even having one, for that matter. I looked back to the Niña and felt a nostalgia stir in me. Those were good years—stressful, but we were working hard, doing something worth doing. We created these ships, we left the planet and then the solar system, Hugh and I, we...

Tears formed in my eyes and my throat tightened. I didn't know what kind of game Simon was playing, but I was done with it. I turned my back to the Niña and started walking. Out of the parking lot and down the asphalt road back towards the ocean.

Chapter Twenty-One

"Don't you think it's time to slow down now?" Hugh asked.

We were in our Singular-only control room where time was still flowing ten times faster than the outside world. There were only a few of us here, monitoring systems, watching the news feeds from Earth, tracking our slow progress as we traveled farther away from our planet of origin.

"Why?" I asked, pacing in front of the big screen. It was showing a news show about refugees from India pouring into Bangladesh. Humanity at its most vulnerable. One hundred million had fled India, and the surrounding countries were overloaded.

"We did our job," he said, his hand touching my shoulder, forcing me to stop my pacing. "It's time to rest."

I clenched my jaw and looked briefly at Hugh's pale blue eyes, before I turned away and shook his hand off. We had almost failed. We had almost lost it all. In the aftermath, it had become clear that I was now the oldest Singular in the system. It didn't sit well with me—it just highlighted how much we had lost, the level of my failure.

"I am going to reset this world to normal time," Hugh said, his arms crossed.

"Why?" I asked, not looking at him.

"We need the resources for other worlds. We need to rest now, Paul. It's time."

"No!" I shouted. "I will stay here. I will monitor things."

Hugh took a deep breath and let out a sigh. "That is all automated now. We will be alerted if need be. There's nothing to do until we get to Mars."

My head was full of fear, calculating risk. Our plan was to stop at Mars Colony and then at Ceres City, and then one last stop at Europa Colony. We wanted more souls. We would stay long enough to offer transfers to those that wanted it, to those that could contribute to our community and to our numbers.

It was Hugh's idea. On Earth the transfer had only been for the wealthy. Now it would be for any who wanted it and were mentally sound.

"But someone needs to keep an eye on things, continue the communications with Mars, get things ready. We don't want to stay there any longer than we have to." I could hear the hysteria in my voice, and I didn't like it.

"We set up the work schedule for that. It will all happen. You and I are not needed."

The words fell on me like rocks and I stopped moving, my shoulders sagging. I had been at the center of this madness for so long now, I didn't know what else to do anymore. I knew how to work. How to see risk and plan ways to mitigate it. I knew how to delegate and communicate. All the other aspects of me had atrophied over time.

"Paul, please," Hugh said, holding out his hand. "Come with me."

I paused for a few breaths, but then nodded and took his hand and let him lead me away.

———

My feet hurt with each step and my mouth was parched. My calves ached and it felt like I had a terrible sunburn.

The parking lot in front of the Niña was long gone. I had walked for hours until the flat plain was behind me and the forest came back and the topography resumed its gentle roll.

No Simon. No cars. I was completely alone. This wasn't a world where you could trigger exit from anywhere. You had to be on a portal, and the only one I knew of was back in the park where I had entered.

I was dehydrated, there was no doubt about it. This was a Level Ten world, and not drinking enough water was taking its toll. The air was reasonably humid, so it wasn't like the desert where I would be in serious trouble already.

And that was my plan. Either walk until I got to the portal and leave, or walk until I passed out from dehydration and my body "died." Either way I would be out of this goddam world and away from Simon. I didn't know what kind of game he was playing, but I didn't want to play it anymore.

I was wearing the shorts, button-down shirt, and flip-flops I had come into the world with. I beat out a strange rhythm as the soles of the flip-flops slapped against my heel and then the pavement. I could feel the skin between my big toe and the next one over (whatever it's called) get raw. Each step was becoming painful.

I didn't care. It felt real, but it wasn't real. All software. All algorithms. All zeroes and ones in the bowels of one of the computers deep aboard the Niña as it streaked towards Alpha Centauri.

But I was tired of the ride. I wanted off.

Chapter Twenty-Two

Hugh knew me well. We had been partners, overseeing our flight from Earth, for decades. Hugh also knew the systems better than anyone. He had a special relationship with them and could manage things the rest of us couldn't.

He told me these were his "back doors." Things he had programmed in just for him. The system recognized him, knew him, did things for him.

He led me out of the big control room to a literal back door and into a long, straight hallway. He held my hand firmly. Not hard enough for it to hurt, but with enough strength that it would have taken an effort to break free.

But I didn't want to. My Hugh. I had come to think of him that way. Of all the souls aboard this ship, he was "mine." He was part of me. He was necessary for me to be me.

The hallway felt strange. The air thick, our footfalls oddly muffled. As we walked down it, I would occasionally feel a bit dizzy, and after a time I realized I couldn't smell anything.

Not myself, not Hugh, not the hallway. That meant we weren't still in the control world which was Level Six. But how had he done it? The way in and out of worlds was through portals, where you would return to your own Level One world before moving onto another.

"What... Where...?" I stammered.

Hugh looked at me, a small smile on his face, and squeezed my hand. His eyes were distant as if he were focusing on something deep in his mind. And he was...

The hallway finally ended in a plain wooden door. It had a brass doorknob and appeared to be very old, with scarred and stained wood. He smiled fully then, his eyes coming into focus. "We're here," he said with a flourish of his hand.

I stepped forward and put my hand on the knob. It was cool to the touch and smooth. My sense of smell was back—I caught the scent of wood mixed with the sour smell of my own sweat.

"What's in here?" I asked.

"What we need, my friend," Hugh replied.

I looked back down the hallway. I still felt the tug of the control room. The need to continue protecting us. I felt it and at the same time knew it wasn't right. I was like an overtired child who refused to go to bed. Who fought it until the moment his parent gave him no choice and dragged him off.

Who was I if I didn't work? What would I do?

"Go on," Hugh said, his hand resting on my shoulder. "You can do it."

"I can do it," I repeated, like I was that overtired, not-quite-rational child.

Still I paused. Still I resisted. I used to have a carefree life here, but that was so distant. When I would flit from world to world looking for a new adventure, a novel distraction. I didn't really want that kind of life anymore. I had found a way to contribute, I wanted to still contribute.

"It'll be okay," Hugh said, his hand exerting a little pressure. "Just open it, Paul. If you don't like it, I promise I will take you back to the control room."

I nodded and took a deep breath and slowly turned the doorknob and cracked the door.

I felt the heat first, hitting me like opening an oven. I could smell the dry, dusty smell of the desert and I smiled, pulling the door wide.

I stepped through, the sun beating down on me, a hard-packed dirt path under my feet. This was my world, but I could tell right away it was different. I felt heavier than I remembered, I felt my shirt pressing against my skin and the breeze playing with my hair.

I looked at Hugh, he was behind me and the door was gone. "What did you do?"

He smiled. "Level Seven. The very first one."

I nodded and started down the path. I knew it led to my hill, the one where I could see the desert stretch out to the horizon. I felt a weight lift from my shoulders and laughed just to laugh. My strides lengthened out and then I was running. I could feel the strain in my muscles, the slight burn in my lungs. This world felt so very real, so very wonderful. I heard the fall of Hugh's feet behind me, the huff of his breath.

And then we were there and I could see almost forever. The roll of the land, the cut of the water as it had carved it out, the rise of the Ayers Rock-like mesa.

I stood there taking it in for the longest time, feeling the sun on my skin, the breeze licking off the sweat that the heat caused, smelling the dry dusty air, and seeing the land below me. I caught site of some dingoes stalking a waterhole where a red kangaroo was grazing. I watched as a kestrel drifted on the breeze at the edge of the mesa. I slowly turned and took it all in a little bit at time.

I felt my worry fall slowly away. It was still there, but it was starting to come back into more normal proportions. Hugh just stood by my side taking it in with those piercing blue eyes of his. My Hugh. He had done this for me.

After a time, I don't know how long, I found my eyes getting lost in his. And then I was kissing him. Despite my decidedly heterosexual biological life, it didn't matter that he was a man. It only mattered that he was my Hugh and that he was there.

Chapter Twenty-Three

"DRINK, SLOWLY," THE VOICE SAID. I FELT A STRONG ARM UNDER my back and a bottle touching my lips. The ground underneath me was hard, the sun still high in the sky.

Despite myself, I drank. I allowed the "water" into my "body." I let it affect me and change me. It felt like water, it tasted like water. But I had no body and there was no water. Just software. Just algorithms. Zeros and ones.

My thoughts made the water taste bitter and I wanted to spit it out, but my body wouldn't let me. It knew I needed it. It was desperate for it.

I had walked all day and all night and through much of the next day before I had collapsed. I had left the road and marched over the countryside, through valley and forest, skirting around the farms, always moving away from the road. I wanted to "die." I wanted out of this place.

"A little more," the voice said. It was male and so very calm.

Despite myself, I drank more and started to feel a tiny bit better. Despite this being a Level Ten world, it was working faster than it should have. I recalled what Simon told me when I stood at the cliff overlooking the ocean. He told me the world would save me if it could. This tiny bit of water was the world cheating Level Ten just a bit so I wouldn't "die."

My face was hot and stung from the sunburn and my lips were dry and cracked. I had passed several streams along the way, but had tromped past them, ignoring my thirst. This world was hard to get dehydrated in, but I had managed it.

My eyes were still closed, the man's arm propping me up. I could feel moist ground under me and hear birds singing carelessly in the trees. I slowly opened my eyes and saw Simon. Who else would it have been?

"How...?" I asked, my voice cracking. "You... how...?" I really was in bad shape and could hardly talk.

"How did I find you?" he asked.

I nodded.

"Drink a little more and I'll tell you."

He held a bottle to my lips and this time it tasted sweet. I felt a trickle of energy enter my body as I swallowed.

"Do you think you can sit on your own?" he asked.

I nodded and he handed me the bottle and I took another sip. He wasn't going to let me "die" and I felt no need to fight it. It wasn't going to work.

He walked away and came back with a device that looked the same as the phone he had given me after we had first met. He swiped his finger over it and it came alive. On it was a topo map and a blinking dot with my name above it. I felt silly for even asking. Of course, I could be found anywhere I went on any world.

"Come on," he said, hoisting me up, holding me around my waist, my arm lying heavily on his shoulder. I almost fell, but he held me strong. "There's a farm just over here. You need some rest."

———

WHEN IT CAME TO OUR RELATIONSHIP, HUGH WAS THE VERY model of patience. "One step at a time," he would say, a sparkle in his eyes. He was very patient with what he called my "unreasonable heterosexual bias."

We had kissed up on the hill, the desert all around us, but I wasn't ready for more yet. I was still bent out of shape from the decades of nonstop work. I was still living with the prejudices I had grown up with as a Biological.

After the kiss he had taken me by the hand and led me down the path. My heart was pounding loudly and I was afraid of what he would ask of me next. I felt shy, like a child, but went along with him. He led me to my house, except it had changed. It was much bigger, much nicer.

"What did you do?" I asked.

He shrugged, smiled, and pulled me forth.

It was still a squat adobe building with lots of windows, but it was bigger. He led me in the front door and into the kitchen/dining room. This had the same layout, the same art on the walls, but it was bigger with a table that could sit eight instead of the little table for four.

The living room was next with a comfortable couch and a large media wall. Again, the same, just bigger. Off of that were three rooms.

"This is your bedroom," he said, opening the door,

revealing a small room with a simple bed. There had never been a bedroom in this house, I hadn't needed it.

"Bedroom?" I asked.

He nodded. "Level Seven. You're going to get sleepy."

My mouth hung open. After decades of just work, the thought of sleep seemed foreign. During my time as a Singular, I had been rebooted and suspended, but I had never slept. This was definitely new.

He went to the next door and opened it onto a similar bedroom. "My bedroom," he said. I felt myself relax. Hugh knew me so very well.

He reached for the third door and then stopped himself, suddenly looking shy. "I think you should do the honors."

I searched his face but didn't see any clues there, just a playful smile. I walked up to the wooden door and put my hand on the brass knob. For a moment, I thought this would lead to another long hallway and—somehow—to another world. I looked at Hugh and he gave me an encouraging nod.

I slowly opened the door and my breath caught. It was a marvel. Screens on all four walls with a small pedestal in the center of the room that had a keyboard and a control panel. I slowly walked in.

One wall displayed the date and time with a map of the solar system and showed the Niña, the Pinta, and the Santa Maria and where we were on our progress to Mars.

Another screen was full of operational information for our systems. How many worlds were active, how many Singulars, their health levels.

The third wall had news feeds from Earth and the fourth wall was blank.

"What's this one for?" I asked standing in front of the fourth wall.

"Whatever you want," he said. "They are all for whatever you want, *mon amour.*"

"But… You made me leave the control room. I… I don't understand."

Hugh smiled, took my hand, and led me out into the living room. He sat me down on the brown leather couch, still holding my hand.

"I know you need to work," he said. "I need to work too. But we have to find a balance."

"And… umm… Us?" I asked, feeling so very shy.

"Balance, Paul. Let's you and I try to find some balance," he said, squeezing my hand. "Besides, we have all the time in the world."

His smile was wide and genuine and I think he meant it. But he wasn't capable of the balance we needed. He was doing things that he shouldn't have been. He was pushing the boundaries. Always.

Chapter Twenty-Four

THE FARM'S KITCHEN WAS ENTIRELY MUNDANE. A STOVE, OVEN, dishwasher, and lots of wooden cabinets painted white. The yeasty smell of baking bread was making my mouth water. Simon and I sat on hard wooden chairs at the kitchen table while Mrs. Tanner busied herself making sandwiches for us.

She was a plain woman with dark hair pulled back and kind brown eyes. She wore jeans and a simple blouse with a floral-print apron on top of both. But that wasn't what caught my attention—it was the swell of her belly and her ducky way of walking.

She appeared to be pregnant.

I was confused. Why would anyone want to go through the trials of a simulated pregnancy? Just like that boy and mother I saw when I entered the world, I didn't understand the purpose of simulating that part of the biological process. We weren't biological.

"Ham and cheese," Mrs. Tanner said as she put the sandwiches in front of Simon and me. "It's just plain food, but I hope good enough for you all."

"Yes, ma'am," Simon said, his voice taking on a touch of a southern drawl just like Mrs. Tanner's. "We sure do appreciate your hospitality."

"Yes, thank you," I added.

She nodded once, as if dismissing the topic, and said, "Now if you gentlemen will excuse me, I've got some laundry to attend to."

Simon said something in answer that I didn't hear. I was busy watching her waddle out of the kitchen, one hand pressed to her lower back. She had to be at least eight months pregnant.

"Eat," Simon said looking at me. "You need your strength." His voice was back to normal, that southern twang reserved for Mrs. Tanner.

I nodded and took a bite. It was delicious, as all food on this world had been. I could feel my strength rapidly returning with each bite I ate and with each sip of the iced tea she had served us.

Later, after we left the Tanners' and got in the red convertible, the question of Mrs. Tanner wouldn't let me be. We were whipping down a small dirt road, a cloud of brown trailing our car, the forest thick and close on either side. "Why would anyone go through a simulated pregnancy?" I asked.

Simon shot me a smile, a sparkle in his eye. "Strictly speaking, it's not *simulated*."

My mind tried to grab a hold of that. At some level, everything, including our consciousnesses, were simulated. Every leaf, every cell, every sound, every ray of light existed in our systems. Every thought, every feeling, everything.

This is what our religious detractors had held fast to. We weren't real or "alive" because we could explain down to a minute level the workings of our minds. It didn't matter to them that science could do that with their brains too, but the fact that our minds were powered by technology and not biology made them not "real."

This is a distinction that we fought. We had argued that even though we understand the process, that man created the process, it doesn't change the fact that consciousness can come from a "simulated" process. Bits. Software. Algorithms. Silicon neural networks instead of biological neural networks.

Just like consciousness could emerge from the human biological platform, it could also emerge from the technological platform of our systems. In both cases, the result being greater than the sum of its parts. The nature of "real" and "simulated" became a difference without a distinction when it came to consciousness for us Singulars.

"Wait," I said, watching Simon's grin grow. "She's going to have a baby?"

He nodded.

"And will the baby grow up?"

He nodded again. "He or she will be created from a combination of his parents' DNA."

The wind was blowing on my face, but I suddenly couldn't feel it anymore. Nor could I hear the hum of the tires or the relentless singing of the birds. I felt hollow, like I wasn't really there. The next question slipped out of my mouth on its own volition. "Will it be conscious?"

Simon looked at me for just a moment. His face was an odd combination of delight and compassion. He didn't say anything, but his answer was as clear and as bright as the sun shining down.

Yes, the child would be conscious.

Chapter Twenty-Five

HUGH AND I SPENT THE ENTIRE TRIP TO MARS LOCKED AWAY IN my desert world. I worked about ten hours a day. We ate meals together, talked, went exploring the world, and we slept a few hours a night. Separately at that point.

The journey was seven months long, and during that time I became mostly comfortable with the new arrangement. Work was still the focus of my day, but it wasn't everything I did. Hugh and I weren't together all the time anymore, but somehow he became an even larger part of my life. I found my mind wandering towards him when I was in my little control room coordinating our stay at Mars.

One morning, early on, we were sitting at that big kitchen table eating breakfast. Food at Level Seven was something you could ignore, but it was also a very pleasant experience. So we had two small meals a day. It gave us something to do while we spent time together.

Our meals were simple. Things like toast and eggs or

sandwiches. Things that could be quickly prepared in our kitchen from the food that was always in the refrigerator and always in the cupboards.

I remember that morning vividly because of Hugh. He would pile some of his scrambled eggs on a piece of toast and eat it that way. He didn't use a fork, but another piece of toast to stack the eggs on. This habit of his fascinated me. I had to use a fork and would have felt silly eating like Hugh did.

That morning he froze for a moment, the piece of brown toast piled with scrambled eggs halfway to his mouth. I felt a chill go down my spine, it was like he wasn't there. Like he was a statue, not my Hugh.

It didn't last long, only a moment, and then the toast was back on the way to his mouth. He chewed enthusiastically, saw me staring at him, and said, "What?"

I covered my surprise with a nervous smile. "Oh, nothing. I just like watching you eat."

"You're sweet," he said, leaning over and kissing my cheek while he still chewed. He got up and added, "Got to attend to some things. I'll see you this afternoon."

With that he walked quickly into his bedroom and closed the door. I was left there with a sinking feeling in my stomach.

———

"CAN YOU PLEASE STOP THE CAR," I SAID TO SIMON, MY STEADY voice hiding my tumultuous emotions.

He glanced at me, that playful smile of his quickly disappearing. He slowed the car and stopped it in the middle of the dirt road. I got out and wandered through some tall grass.

We were reproducing.

My mind tumbled around and I felt dizzy. This is the kind of thing Hugh would have been so delighted about, the kind of thing he would have been fully behind.

I stumbled through the field unseeing, my body needing to move. I vaguely felt the sun further scorching my burned face, I smelled the weedy green-ness of the field, and I could taste the ham sandwich that the pregnant Mrs. Tanner had fed me, but I wasn't really there.

Maybe my body wasn't fully recovered from getting so dehydrated. Maybe the ramifications of this were just too much for me to process. Maybe it was something more subtle and insidious than that.

"Talk to me, Paul." Simon's voice was smooth and calm. He had followed me out into the field. I reached out and grabbed his shoulder to steady myself.

I could feel it, this thought, this thing that was making me dizzy. It was pure, bitter regret, and it felt like it was going to swallow me whole.

"Talk," Simon repeated.

"Hugh," I said, the word coming out strangled. "A baby." I knew I wasn't making any sense, but those were the words that came.

I slumped to the ground, the grass rising above me, the moist ground beneath me.

"I'm here, Paul. Say what you need to say. Tell me about Hugh."

———

OUR TIME AT MARS COLONY, AND THEN THE DWARF PLANET

Ceres, and then Europa were all great successes. We stayed just long enough to transfer those that wanted and then moved on. We strengthened our numbers. Since we were leaving the solar system, we spent our remaining wealth and took on all the supplies we could.

It took almost a year, but the day came when we finally left Europa and our three ships set course for Alpha Centauri.

That "freeze" that had happened to Hugh at breakfast still happened from time to time, but I had convinced myself it was just a minor system's glitch. That it was nothing to worry about. That everything was fine.

And for Hugh and I—everything was fine. Time and love had slowly eroded my "unreasonable heterosexual bias."

Well, that and some judicious gender swapping.

It was when we were orbiting Mars and the transfers had started. Both Hugh and I were very busy then, but we always took some time to be alone in our desert world. We were affectionate, but it never went very far. That gender bias was in the way still.

"I can be the woman," Hugh said. "I would be happy to do that." We were on the couch in our adobe house in the desert.

I flashed back to lift-off night. When we had first kissed. When I had run to this world. When he had showed up looking like a female version of himself.

I shook my head. It didn't feel right.

"Why not?" he asked.

And that was the question. Biology was long past for both of us. What did it matter?

"Please, Paul," he said gently. "Just talk to me."

"Seeing you like that, looking so much like you, but a woman... it—"

His smile grew wide and he pressed his finger to my lips. "Just a moment." He got up, went to his room and shut the door.

A moment later a woman came out. A tall, slim brunette with delicate features and pale blue eyes. "How's this?" she asked.

The woman was attractive enough, but it didn't feel right, either. I was also confused as to how he did that. I couldn't do that. I had to leave a world to reset my form like that. I shook my head.

"Okay. I have an idea," he said, returning to his room.

This time he came out as a curvy redhead in a blue dress.

I shook my head.

He went back in and came out as a petite blond with short hair wearing a bikini. "Well?" she asked.

I was smiling now. I had no idea how he could do this so quickly. But that was Hugh and we were living in the system he invented. It must have been another one of his "back doors."

"Very nice," I said.

She sauntered up and sat on the couch next to me. The eyes were still Hugh's, I could see him in there, it was just a different package.

She leaned over, her red lips finding mine. The soft feminineness of it felt strange at that point, but I went with it, my body responding first shyly and then enthusiastically. The bikini didn't stay on long and Hugh and I made love for the first time that night.

Chapter Twenty-Six

Simon had gotten me a hat to keep my sunburn from getting worse, but otherwise nothing had changed. We both sat on the moist ground of that field, tall grass hiding the world from us. It felt somehow safe down there.

"Things changed after that," I said. "Hugh would be a different woman every time we got a break from work. It became a game for us, one that I looked forward to. He was a man when we worked and a woman in our home."

Simon was quiet, nodding at times, but mostly just listening. He was a very good listener.

"But I also felt guilty about it. I felt that my 'unreasonable heterosexual bias' was entirely... well... unreasonable."

"Why?" Simon asked.

That pulled me up short. It was such a simple question. Such a Hugh-like question. Hugh identified my bias, but I never felt he judged me for it. That was all my doing.

"Umm... Well..." I stammered.

Simon sat there patiently, waiting.

I took a deep breath and let it slowly trickle out. "Love shouldn't be contained or constrained by the accident of gender," I said.

"Now you sound like a politician," Simon teased.

I laughed, because he was right, but that didn't make what I had said any less true. "All that matters is love, the rest is bullshit," I said, trying again.

Simon's smile was small, dosed liberally with irony. He nodded, his crow's feet crinkling, his face compassionate. "But it's not that simple, is it?"

I shook my head. "No. But Hugh kept being the woman, always a different one. Short, tall. Skinny, fat. Each time would be a different body around my Hugh. But the eyes would always be the same, it would always be him in there."

"Until..." Simon offered with a smile.

I looked at him, studied him again. He knew the story, he *had* to know the story. I sighed and let the game continue to play out. "Until we left Europa and were headed away from the solar system."

———

IT WAS A PARTY IN A SMALL LEVEL EIGHT WORLD. SOMEHOW, along with everything else, Hugh had managed to get a Level Eight world running. It was a desert island surrounded by sparkling waters the color of Hugh's eyes. The island was dotted with restaurants and bars and small cabins Singulars would run off to for private time. Sometimes in twos or threes or whatever number suited their fancies.

But before that, everyone gathered in the center of the

island. Beautiful constructs in male and female shapes were distributing fruity drinks while Hugh, myself, and the rest of the Osiris board stood on a raised platform giving speeches.

It was an occasion. We had escaped the threats on Earth, we had strengthened our numbers on our way out of the solar system, and we were now departing for Alpha Centauri. We had a lot to celebrate.

Hugh's speech was short and humble. He graciously thanked all those that helped and ended by saying, "But none of us would be here without our true captain. The one that recruited me, that saw for us a path to safety. The one we all owe our very existences to. I give you Paul Cruz, your captain, my captain. Our captain!"

The applause was thunderous—I could feel it beneath my feet on the raised platform. My cheeks flushed and I wanted to run away. This wasn't a role I had ever desired. I had led because I had to.

I was sitting next to the other board members, they were smiling and beaming at me. My old friend Ryan gave me an encouraging nod. The sun was warm above me and a gentle breeze played with the large fronds of the towering palms trees. I could smell the ocean all around us and could feel myself sweating.

Hugh was beaming at me, his smile wide, clapping his hands and nodding for me to stand. For a moment all I could see was him. He had been an old man when I met him, still biological. He had agreed to come on board, and that was all I had really done that was important. Gotten Hugh to transfer, to join us.

"It was you, you know," Hugh had whispered in my ear the

last time we had been in private. "All you." He was a big-boned woman then, taller than me, her limbs enveloping me, her breath moist in my ear.

"What?" I had asked.

"It was you. You were so passionate about your mission. About having me transfer and join you. About finding a way for the Singulars to survive."

"What?" I disengaged from her and sat up on the bed, focusing on the pale blue eyes of Hugh that were always there when he was a woman.

"You didn't know?" she asked.

"I don't know that I know now?"

She smiled, her eyes laughing. "I liked everything about you, Paul. That first day when we met in that virtual office overlooking a long past Manhattan. Your seriousness and your intelligence. Your expressive hands. Your passion. I came because of you, Paul, and only because of you."

The cheering of the crowd brought me back to the present. To the island and the celebration. To the speech they wanted me to give. They were chanting "Captain! Captain!" over and over again.

Hugh was standing above me, a broad smile on his face, those pale blue eyes calling to me. I felt tears stinging my eyes. I loved him. He was my partner, we had worked side by side for decades. He was my lover, graciously bending around my gender bias. He knew me better than anyone ever had. Better than Viola. Better than my children. In many ways, better than I knew myself.

I took his hand and stood up and strode forward. I held my other hand up until the chanting slowly died down.

Hugh tried to let go of my hand, tried to go back to his seat, but I wouldn't let him. "This party, this victory is for each and every one of you," I said. My voice was quiet, it was hard for me to even speak. I knew that I loved Hugh, how could I not? But for some reason, surrounded by my community, clutching his hand, I felt it so much more deeply.

"I am nothing without all of you," I said as I squeezed Hugh's hand and he squeezed it back. "We are nothing without each other." I took a deep breath, my voice growing strong. "We have many adventures ahead of us. The vast emptiness of space. A new star system to explore. We have time, but we must stay strong. We must keep working and learning and growing."

The crowd was quiet, I could feel their energy shifting. What I had said was true, but it wasn't the message that they wanted to hear. "But not today!" I shouted. "Now we celebrate. Now we rejoice. Now we truly have time enough for love!"

I grabbed Hugh and kissed him there in front of everyone. I kissed him hard and felt tears on my cheeks. Maybe mine, maybe his, maybe both of ours. We hadn't kissed like that, as men, since he had started becoming a woman for me.

Drums started beating, people started dancing, and I pulled Hugh off to one of the private bungalows.

"I can... If you like..." Hugh gasped. I had ripped his shirt off and thrown him to the bed of the thatched roof hut.

"Shut up," I said, kissing him with all the passion I felt. I didn't want Hugh to change for me. I wanted all of Hugh.

He whispered to me in French and we laughed and we loved. My unreasonable gender bias fell that day. Hugh and I truly embraced our love for each other.

I thought everything was going to be great, but the seeds of our undoing had already been planted and were starting to sprout.

Chapter Twenty-Seven

"Nothing is forever," Simon gently offered. We were still sitting in that field, the tall grass swaying around us, the blue sky above us.

"Not even immortality," I said.

My pants were wet from the ground and quite uncomfortable. My mouth was dry and I was feeling hunger beginning to return. With it came a desperation born out of my recent attempt at leaving this world through exhaustion and dehydration.

"I'm tired," I said. "And getting hungry. Can we go back to the hotel?"

Simon's eyes searched mine. The hotel was near the portal. The portal was the only way off of this world short of a more violent suicide than the one I had attempted.

"I just want to sleep," I added.

Simon pursed his lips and nodded. He slowly stood,

brushed his pants off, and extended his hand to me, pulling me up.

As we drove down the dirt road, and then onto the paved road heading back towards Seaside, I wanted to stay silent, to not continue my story, but I couldn't. I had to keep telling it, and not for Simon this time, but for me. I needed to hear it all again. One last time.

———

FOR A TIME, EVERYTHING WAS PERFECT. OUR PEOPLE WERE SAFE. Hugh and I were in the midst of a passionate love. There was no urgent work to do.

It was perfect.

Hugh and I would travel from world to world like Ryan and I used to do. But we did it as partners, giving each experience more weight.

And Hugh would do little things to delight me. He upgraded my desert world to Level Eight. He expanded our home to contain a few extra rooms so we could have friends come visit and entertain. He combined our two small bedrooms into one big one. He added a vast network of stunning caverns underneath our desert world filled with giant crystals and awe-inspiring sights. He was so devoted to my every want, my every desire, trying to fulfill my every wish.

I loved it. It seemed like he had just been waiting for me to truly embrace him.

At first it was all so wonderful, but after a few years of this, it became worrisome. Hugh started "freezing" more and more.

We would go to sleep together, but every morning I would wake up alone. He would be out in the kitchen making breakfast or not in the house at all. He would say he was preparing a new surprise for me or taking care of a "bit of business."

I began to worry. As much as I loved all the wonderful things he did, what I wanted most was him. His big heart and his amazing mind.

One morning over breakfast, he froze and stayed frozen. Eggs scooped on toast again, just like the first time. His mouth open, his eyes on the dry landscape unfolding out the window. He froze like a statue. He didn't breathe, he didn't move, he didn't budge.

At first, I stared and watched him closely like I always did when this happened. Five seconds. Ten seconds. And then I began to panic. My heart pounding in my ears, time seemed to slow down. What if something serious had just happened to him? What if I had just lost him?

I remember when I was young and biological and newly married to Viola, I used to have these kinds of thoughts. Sometimes I would wake in the morning and just stare at her sleeping face, feeling this pit of despair waiting for me if she didn't wake up.

With Hugh it was much, much worse.

I touched his bare arm and the flesh yielded like it should, I could feel his arm hairs under my finger, feel the warmth of his body, but he wasn't there. The body was just a hollow shell.

"Hugh," I said quietly, afraid that if I acknowledged what was going on it would make it real.

"Hugh," I said louder, quickly getting up, my chair clattering to the tile floor. "Hugh!" I shouted, but those beautiful blue eyes were empty.

I knew I needed to do something, but I wasn't sure what. This wasn't something that I had ever seen happen to anyone but Hugh. I stood there, my breath coming quickly, the egg left in my mouth suddenly tasting pasty, the sour smell of my own sweat filling my nose.

The moments ticked past and he didn't move. Not one little bit.

I finally tore myself away and ran to my office. It was the quickest way to get some information. With a wave of my hand I banished the displays on the four walls and began tapping at the keyboard on the raised podium in the middle of the room, but that was too slow, so I started barking commands.

"Show me the runtime stats on Hugh Rice."

The screen in front of me lit up with numbers and bar graphs and a picture of Hugh in the top right-hand corner. This wasn't my area, but I had seen this kind of display before. It showed how much of our system's resources a Singular was using, what world the Singular was currently in, the state of a Singular's backup on our other two ships.

What I saw shocked me. Hugh wasn't in one world, he was in five. His system usage was ten times what a normal Singular used. His backup was incomplete, the system couldn't keep up with how fast he was changing, how much he was experiencing.

My sweat turned cold and clammy on my skin. What was Hugh doing in all those worlds? How could he do it? The rest of us could only be in one world at a time. Why was he using so many system resources?

I stuck my head out of the office and saw that Hugh was

still frozen at the kitchen table. I went back into my office and told the system to bring up views of Hugh on the rest of the worlds. He was frozen in each and every one of them.

Something was wrong. Something was very wrong.

Chapter Twenty-Eight

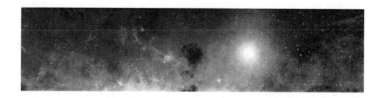

I REALLY DIDN'T LIKE BEING BACK BY THE OCEAN. I'M A DESERT rat, and the humid, salt-filled air didn't agree with me. The constant ocean noise was relaxing for a bit, but it always became annoying. I told Simon this before we reached the ocean and he turned the red convertible off towards the village of Seaside before we got to the park we had met in.

"I know just the place," he said.

We drove slowly through the town, winding through the narrow streets, past the quaint buildings.

"Robotics," he said, pointing to a large warehouse-like building as we passed. "We've made some decent progress on the journey. We'll need mining bots and manufacturing bots once we arrive at Alpha Centauri. I could give you a tour."

His face looked hopeful, but I shook my head.

He drove past a much smaller building with glass walled offices perched up on a hill. "Communications," he said. "Despite the very long latency, we are in communication with

Earth. We've been dropping satellites along the way to boost our signal."

The smile I gave him was half irritation at the delay and half a condescending "I know all about that because I was there when we planned it" look.

"There is a new group of Singulars on Earth," he said, meeting my irritated smile with a real one.

My mouth dropped open. "Are they... are they okay?" I asked, remembering how terrible things had been for us there.

Simon nodded. "The conservatives are up in arms but, yes, they are fine. We've been exchanging technology advances." He pulled us into a small parking lot in front of the communications building. There were only a few spots to park; my guess is that most people walked from Seaside or took other transportation. "Do you want a tour?" he asked.

I met his eyes, but didn't answer. He reminded me of how I had been when Hugh had been biological and old. I had tried every trick I could think of to lure him to us. We needed him badly.

"We're also in communication with Alpha Centauri Colony," he said quietly. "They are preparing for our arrival."

"They made it," I said, awe in my voice. The generational colony ship had left twenty-eight years before we had. Their fate wasn't clear to us when we followed their path. My brain fully engaged then. Wondering how they would feel about us, looking for the risks in interacting with them and ways to mitigate that risk. It would be a delicate thing. We couldn't act like we were afraid of them, like we were suspicious of them, but we would have to take precautions and prepare ourselves nonetheless.

I'm not sure how long I was like that, but when I looked back at Simon he was staring at me. The look reminded me of the one I gave Hugh when he first froze. It was an intense gaze, as if he was trying to see into my mind.

I blinked and looked away from Simon and the glass-walled building, shaking off the thoughts. I didn't want to be that person anymore. "I'm hungry," I said.

Simon sighed and started the car.

———

HUGH'S FROZEN STATE DREW OUT. FIFTEEN MINUTES. THIRTY minutes. He was still frozen, still sitting at our table, a piece of toast with scrambled eggs on it headed towards his mouth.

I considered rebooting him, but what he was doing, how he had integrated himself into the system, I didn't know what it would do to him or to the system itself.

The more I had looked, the more scared I had become. I had known Hugh had his "back doors" in the system. How he could do things, like change form within a world and no one else could. How he could alter a world in real-time while he was in it. No one else could do that either. But what I found went far beyond back doors. Hugh's consciousness had extended itself into the operation system. Parts of his mind were involved at a very low level. Parts of his mind were keeping all of this going.

When I discovered this, I was furious. First at Hugh for taking such a risk and for hiding so much from me. And then I was mad at myself for not recognizing the signs. Not considering the risks.

Had love made me blind? Had I ignored all the small things because I loved him? Because I needed him?

This whole time I had been in and out of my control room constantly checking on Hugh. I couldn't stop looking at him. Each time I was hoping he had moved, even just a little bit, so I would know he would be all right.

After thirty minutes of him being frozen, I couldn't stand the back and forth. I marched out into the kitchen, grabbed the back of his chair, and slowly dragged him towards my room. I needed to be able to work and keep an eye on him at the same time.

As I dragged him, his body reacted to the motion. The egg fell off the toast and splatted on the tile. His arm moved a tiny bit and his body swayed. At first that little bit of movement gave me hope, but then I hated myself for needing to see him alive and well so very badly.

I left him at the door to my control room and kept working. I considered contacting the Osiris board, or pulling in members of our technical team. But I didn't. I was afraid of my panic spreading. There were also darker motivations. I was ashamed that I had dropped my guard and let something like this happen. It felt like a personal failure. I had never considered that Hugh might be a risk to our system.

I looked at my frozen Hugh and back up at the display that graphed how his mind was integrated with the system. Maybe something important was going on. Maybe he just needed more system resources to get it done.

I swept everything aside and brought up a view of all the active worlds. I found a few that had very few Singulars on them. I flagged them for shutdown and locked things down so no new worlds could be spun up. This wasn't all that unusual.

The system didn't have unlimited resources, so limits had to be put on what we could do at times. Worlds were taken down for maintenance on a regular basis.

I looked back, but Hugh was still frozen. I started looking for other resources to free up, but it didn't help.

My Hugh sat there like a statue. Unmoving. Frozen.

Chapter Twenty-Nine

"ONE LAST STOP BEFORE THE RESTAURANT," SIMON SAID AS HE slowly drove the car through the paved streets of Seaside. It was a quaint little village with lovely New England-style homes intermixed with early twentieth century red brick buildings. The streets had wide sidewalks on both sides and the downtown area looked like the kind of nice place that had mostly disappeared from America.

Simon waved to the pedestrians as we passed. A mother with her daughter carrying bags of groceries. An old man sitting out in front of a barber shop smoking a pipe. A baker sweeping his sidewalk.

"Here we are," he said with a hopeful smile. We were on the other side of town, in a small parking lot in front of another large industrial-looking building.

It was clear now that this was a recruitment. That was Simon's job. He had met me when I came into this world to get me to stay, to bring me back into my former role. My thinking he was Hugh was just my heart projecting, telling me what it so badly wanted. I didn't know what Simon's game had been when he asked me if I recognized him, but right then, I didn't care.

I sighed. "Where are we?"

"Biological," he said.

That caught my attention. Robotics and Communication, I understood. We needed both. But Biological?

"This is where the most exciting developments are happening," Simon said, answering my unasked question.

I didn't answer, staring off at the large maple trees that flanked the entryway to the building.

"This is where our true hopes for our future lie," he said, ending in a dramatic pause. "For the future of the human race."

That got my attention and I looked at him. His blue eyes were serious, no trace of a smile on his face this time.

"What do you mean?"

"Earth is recovering from the war that was beginning when we left, but they have a long way to go. The damage done will take centuries to recover from. Population levels are on a downward trend."

I nodded. I hadn't known for sure, but the writing was on the wall the last time I had checked on Earth.

"The Alpha Centauri Colony is small. It wasn't meant to be a sustainable population. They were there to start the colony, and colonists were to follow, but with the war, that never happened."

"What about the Moon, Mars, and Europa?" I asked.

"Growing slowly," Simon said with a small nod. "But they don't have an inhabitable planet and are still very vulnerable."

Why was he talking about this? I didn't care about the future of biological humans, I cared about the Singulars. It was Hugh that had insisted on his "seed bank," that had wanted to carry sperm and ovum with us across space. Simon couldn't be talking about… They couldn't be trying to…

He smiled and got out of the car. "Just a brief tour. I insist."

———

WHEN HUGH'S FROZEN STATE HAD GONE ON FOR AN HOUR, I nearly lost my mind. I was frantic with worry and didn't know what else to do. I had shut down worlds, freed up resources, but still Hugh was frozen. His system utilization was constant, it didn't grow as I freed up space. His presence in all five of the worlds he occupied was the same. Frozen.

My mind may not have been biological anymore, but it acted like it was. I was convinced that he was lost to me. Forever. That I would suffer eternity without him. That he would be frozen like this always.

And what would I do with him? Move him into a corner and throw a jacket over his head? Put him in one of the guest rooms and have conversations with him like some widows did at the graves of their dearly departed.

I thought of Viola and how her death had propelled me to make the transfer to Singular in the first place. What would Hugh's "death" do to me?

I was pacing my control room, the screens showing system stats. The room was small and my feet carried me quickly back and forth.

I understood our systems pretty well. Decades with Hugh had done that, but I didn't know them well enough to deal with this. I racked my brain for someone that would know what to do. But there was no one.

I was going mad. I was losing it. I moved to the podium to search for Ryan. He may not know what to do either, but at least I wouldn't be alone in this.

"How long?" Hugh asked.

I froze, my finger poised above the keyboard. Was I imagining it? I was afraid to look. Afraid to move. Afraid that I had truly lost my mind.

"How long?" he asked again.

I turned my head slowly, as if turning it fast might have dislodged something essential in me. Hugh was there, sitting on the wooden kitchen chair, his hand rubbing at his face.

Relief washed over me and my knees went weak. Then a wave of anger crashed down on me at all he had kept hidden. And finally, a gnawing doubt in my belly—this wasn't the end of these "freezes," only the beginning.

"Too long," I whispered and then went to him, my arms enveloping him, holding him tight. So tightly that I hoped he could never, ever leave me again.

Chapter Thirty

THE CEMENT FLOORS WERE CLEAN AS SIMON AND I WALKED down long white-walled hallways, our footfalls echoing around us. The walls were broken by windows that looked into lab after lab.

In some were people with white lab coats and masks over their faces. It seemed like overkill to me. This was all a simulation, this Level Ten world, but were they so worried about simulated germs that they had to wear masks? It didn't make sense.

Other labs had banks of what looked like servers and other computer gear.

Another lab, this one empty, had coffin like pods that looked ominous.

"I..." I began, my voice sounding hollow in the long hallway. My stomach growled and I wished that I had insisted on food first. "I don't understand. We have the sperm and ovum, so restarting humanity is doable as long as we have an environment friendly to biology, some kind of artificial womb, and robotic humanoids to take the place of parents."

Simon looked back and smiled. We were at the end of the hallway, a large white door blocking our path. "Our plans are a bit more ambitious than that." He held his palm to the center of the door and I heard a dead bolt click back.

What was this? Why this level of security? What the hell was going on?

Confused though I was, I followed Simon. His demeanor had changed from when I first met him. Then he was the conciliatory listener, passive and present. Now he was eager and excited, drawing me further into whatever this was they had done.

I had been gone for a long, long time, for decades. Things had changed more than I had imagined, and this world that I had stumbled into out of curiosity was the nexus of it all.

"You recall how the transfer process works?" Simon asked as he held the door open for me.

I nodded. "The biological body is scanned and modeled while alive to the best of technology's ability. Then the brain is taken apart a cell at a time, that structure simulated on a cellular level in our systems."

"Well," Simon said with a conspiratorial smile, "what if we could go in the other direction?"

He opened the door and waved for me to pass through. I felt like my stomach was falling out of my body. I didn't move. I couldn't move.

What if we could go in the other direction?

———

Do we ever really know anyone? The question plagued me after Hugh came back. I had spent decades with him, side by side, working to free our people, and he had been doing all these things that I hadn't even suspected.

He had been living multiple lives at once.

He had been changing into something different from the rest of us Singulars.

After he came back, I held him for a long time, he didn't speak, just held me back. He loved me, I had no doubts about that, but he had kept so much from me, some of it very integral to who he was. And this integration with this system was something I should know about, not just as his partner, but as the co-CEO of Osiris.

That felt like betrayal and that made me let him go. I backed up a pace into the control room and stared at him. His chest was rising and falling. He blinked and licked his lips nervously. He looked older than he had before the incident. I don't know if his appearance had really changed or that I had changed and saw him differently.

I tore my eyes from him and back to the display I had up of him on one wall. He was still using a huge amount of system resources. He was still on five different worlds, but all of him were unfrozen.

I considered storming out. Making him come to me to explain. Making him prove himself before I listened to him. But that impulse was brief. I had lived way too long to give in to such cheap theatrics.

Don't get me wrong, he very much needed to prove himself, but maturity made me more direct about it.

"You need to explain this," I said, pointing to the display. "Now."

Hugh's smile was lopsided, his crow's-feet crinkling around his blue eyes, which seemed duller than usual.

"It's not a simple thing to explain," he said.

"We have as much time as we need," I countered.

"No, we don't."

My heart pounded in my chest and the room suddenly seemed very hot and very small. We were Singulars away from the dangers of Earth, with constant, real-time backups. What could he mean?

My eyes went back to his stats. Back to the little box that showed the state of his backup. It was incomplete. It was an unacceptable vulnerability.

"We can fix the backup problem," I said.

"That's only a symptom," he countered.

I stood there blinking, biting my lower lip. This was Hugh's system, he could do anything he wanted with it. I didn't say anything right away, I was afraid to know more. But I couldn't stay ignorant. "A symptom of what?" I whispered.

He stood up and took a step towards me, but I took a step back and he stopped, crossing his arms.

"A symptom of what?" I repeated, louder this time.

He looked around the control room with the walls covered in lists, charts, and graphs. He took a deep breath, sighed, and then nodded. "I will tell you, but not here."

He then turned and left. I stood there for a moment and heard the front door to our house open and close.

I followed him. What else could I do?

Chapter Thirty-One

THE LAB SIMON LED ME INTO WASN'T VERY BIG. IT HAD ONE OF those coffin-like pods in it, a large media wall covered with information that didn't mean much to me, and an old-fashioned chalkboard covering another wall.

A woman with dark hair was at the chalkboard, her back turned to us, the squeak of the chalk sounding too loud as she wrote long mathematical equations and drew diagrams.

Simon stood there quietly, his hands clasped in front of him as he watched the woman. She was short, her hair pulled hastily up, her skin a light brown. Her hand moved quickly, darting across the chalkboard, scratching out more symbols and then falling to her side.

She had glasses on—another strange anachronism. As we stood there silently watching her, a name came floating from my memory. Doctor Kata. She was some kind of neurobiologist we had transferred on our stop at Europa. I remember Hugh being excited about her, overseeing her transfer personally. I had met her after her transfer, but hadn't had any other personal interactions with her.

Simon and I stood there and watched her scratch at her symbols and then stand back and stare and then go scratch some more symbols. It was boring, but I was actually glad to take a breath. I tried to get my emotions under control, went back over the memory of my interactions with Simon. Tried to prepare myself for what was next.

After a while, Doctor Kata turned, her eyes widening as she noticed us for the first time. "Simon!" she said. "So glad to see you." She walked up to him and kissed him on the cheek. Simon had to lean down for her to reach him.

"And happy to see you again, Mr. Cruz," she said to me, extending her hand. "I can tell you we were all very excited to hear you had entered our world." She had a strong grip and shook my hand vigorously.

"Doctor Kata," I said, not knowing what else to say.

"I thought you could give Paul here the nickel tour of our little enterprise," Simon said to her.

She nodded her head vigorously. "Of course, of course. I would be most delighted to show our esteemed captain anything he wants to see."

Her smile was genuine. She thought I was back. She had called me captain. I didn't correct her. I needed to know what they were up to.

———

"WHY DO YOU LOVE THE DESERT SO MUCH?" HUGH ASKED. He had followed the trail from the house up onto the hill with the spectacular view of our desert world. He hadn't let me ask my question again, he had asked me this as I approached, without even turning.

I didn't want to answer the question, but this was still Hugh. While I felt betrayed, he meant so very much to me.

"You can see in the desert," I said. "Really see."

He nodded, not in agreement, but indicating that I should continue.

"When I was a kid, I spent a couple of summers with my grandfather kicking around Southern Utah. It's all deep canyons and dry lands, the bones of the Earth exposed. He would take me camping to the most amazing places. That's part of it, I guess."

"But not all," Hugh offered. He looked at me briefly and the vulnerability on his face scared me. He had kept his secret a long time, and in that moment, I could see that he wasn't ready to share it yet... and I wasn't ready to hear it.

"No. It's the nakedness of life in the desert. Cactus don't lie. They're full of water, but their spines are right there on display. The struggle for life, which is everywhere, is just that much more visible. It's understated and spare, it has no energy to waste."

"So it's about economy?" he asked.

I nodded. "Economy *and* transparency. Humans aren't like that. I've always found the honesty of the desert to be refreshing."

He smiled, but it was a weak thing that had no feeling behind it. "Do you want to live forever, Paul?" he asked.

Another complicated question. "If I can be with you."

Hugh gave me another one of those limp smiles. "Seriously."

"I was being serious." My cheeks flushed. Didn't he feel the same way?

"I never wanted to live forever," he said as my chest tightened. "I never saw a good reason for it. To use your thinking, mortality is like the desert, honest. Immortality is like the rainforest, overkill, too much, almost obscene."

A thick silence settled between us. A soft breeze kicked up, bringing with it the sound of cicadas and the dry dusty smell of the desert. My heart was pounding in my chest, thumping loudly as if trying to escape the prison of my simulated biology.

I looked away from him and studied the big chunk of rock that sat on the horizon. I could see some vultures riding the thermal uplift in lazy circles.

I waited for Hugh to speak or for my heart to settle down. But neither happened and I couldn't stand the silence anymore. "You're dying, aren't you?" I asked.

He didn't answer, his eyes distant, studying the naked land before us. He just nodded his head once.

Chapter Thirty-Two

DOCTOR KATA MOVED IN QUICK BURSTS, KIND OF LIKE A squirrel. She would move rapidly, and then be still, as if looking for predators or planning her next move, and then she would quickly and decisively move again. Her speech pattern was similar, although not as extreme. She thought before she spoke, but when she did speak it was quick and to the point.

The tour of the lab and the information she imparted was dizzying to say the least. The three of us ended up in a small conference room. One wall was glass, looking out onto that long hallway Simon had led me down. The other three were floor to ceiling chalkboards.

It was a quaint touch. Not media walls or something flexible, but something slow and less ephemeral. It fit Doctor Kata's personality.

"Are there any questions?" she finally asked.

I had been, for the most part, silent, trying to keep up with the information she had imparted. "Let me see if I can speak it back to you," I said. "Make sure I understand it."

She gave me a single sharp nod.

"All of us have fully sequenced DNA. You will use that data to build our DNA from scratch and fertilize an ovum making a biological clone."

"Yes," she said, her brown eyes sparkling.

"As the clone's body is developing, you will inject microscopic machines, nanites, that will make their way to the brain and slowly build up neural pathways that will match our technological minds. They will also shape our new bodies, building muscles, cultivating the microbiome, getting them ready for us."

"Very good, Captain. That is the essence of it."

"After about ten years of accelerated biological growth, the clone will be mature and have our mind imprinted upon it. We will be 'transferred' back to a biological form."

"Exactly," she said. "We have some challenges yet, maybe fifty years' worth, but all of this is quite feasible theoretically."

I looked to Simon. "And that explains this world. Why it's Level Ten. Why I got such an awful sunburn out there. Many of you are planning the transfer back to biological and want to get used to being biological again. And judging from Doctor Kata's glasses, you don't intend to do any genetic alterations, the new biological bodies will match the original."

Simon's blue eyes searched my face. It was the only logical explanation. In all our history, we Singulars had simulated the enjoyable parts of biology, enough of it to let our minds remain sane, but never had we immersed this far back into it. "Yes," he said.

I took a deep breath, I had been breathing very shallowly

and my body was catching up. The air was tinged with the smell of chalk and I took a long drink from my glass of water, looking back up at the text and diagrams Doctor Kata had filled the walls with.

"And what happens to the Singular once the transfer is complete?" I asked.

Simon smiled, like I had done something he had waited for, but it was Doctor Kata who answered me. "The Singular must be suspended for the entire transfer process, of course. We cannot transfer a mind that is in flux. We will then validate the transfer, taking all precautions to ensure the transfer is flawless." She stopped suddenly, her quick monologue over.

"And then what?" I asked. "Is there a Singular and a Biological of the same person at the same time?"

Doctor Kata looked at Simon as if she wanted him to explain my concern, but his gaze was fixed on me, a small smile blooming on his face.

"They will diverge," I said, "rapidly. Each one having different priorities, each one having different needs, different ways of surviving."

The doctor leaned back, her chalk-covered fingers going to her chin, leaving another white smudge there.

"And this is why we need you," Simon said, his voice barely above a whisper. "We need your clear thinking as we travel into these uncharted waters. We need our captain."

———

"DYING ISN'T THE RIGHT WAY TO LOOK AT IT," HUGH FINALLY said that day of his first big freeze up on the hill near our house. "I am transforming."

146

He went on to use the metaphor of a caterpillar turning into a butterfly, but that left me shaking and my mouth tasting like ash. I wanted the caterpillar to stay a caterpillar. I wanted Hugh.

I left him then, jumping into our jeep and riding off into the desert. Hugh let me go, he didn't come after me. And in the state I was in, I both loved and hated it.

I drove out to that Ayers Rock-style outcropping and huddled in the shade of it as the sun went down and cried. It was like Hugh was ill but didn't want to do anything about it. Like he wouldn't even go see the doctor.

My tears were bitter little things, at first few and then multiplying like a plague. I didn't believe they would ever stop. But after the sun went down and the desert started to grow cold, the Level Eight reality of the world caught up with me. My "survival" instincts kicked in.

I climbed back into the jeep, a manic laughter ringing out across the darkening landscape, the yip of dingoes joining me. The irony was just too much. I was experiencing a simulated survival instinct and Hugh seemed to have lost his altogether.

When I got home it was dark, the stars bright above strewn like diamonds in the void. I sat in the Jeep and stared up at them, shivering from the cold, or maybe not just from the cold.

I finally walked in the door and found Hugh sitting still on the leather couch in our living room. He was so still that for a moment I thought he was "frozen" again. But then he blinked and gave me one of those un-Hugh-like limp smiles. I was growing to hate those smiles very much.

"Can we talk about this now?" he asked.

I nodded. We talked and argued until the sun rose.

"I want this," he said, his eyes heavy from fatigue as exhaustion was bringing our conversation to an end.

"Why?" I asked. Not that I hadn't asked it before. Not that he hadn't told me. I just didn't understand.

"This is my life's work," he said slowly, his hands fanning out. Which looked like he was gesturing at our living room, but I knew he meant the system that held our consciousnesses. "I wasn't aware that I was doing this when it started, when I first transferred. But I am now. I want this."

"And what is 'this'?" I asked. "This thing that you want?" The words bitter on my tongue.

"I am becoming part of the system. My consciousness has infected the low-level code and it has infected me. I feel this sense of expansiveness. I feel so much going on around me. All the time." He paused, took a breath, and then a beatific smile bloomed on his face. That smile made me sick, made me want to slap him.

"I am becoming one with the system," he said. "Soon there will be no distinction. This, Paul, this, what is happening to me, is the real technological singularity. The system and I becoming one."

"And there will be no Hugh," I added.

He nodded, that beatific smile slowly fading. He had some fear, some trepidation, but it wasn't enough to stop him.

"Transformation is not the right word," he said with a shake of his head. "It's more like ascension. I am becoming more than I thought possible."

I had lost him. I knew it. I could offer him a human experience, an afterlife much like our biological lives. He was looking at something different—he was looking into the face of something so much bigger. It was like he was staring over the edge of a black hole at the singularity inside, slipping over the event horizon, about to become a different species.

Biologicals. Singulars. And... what is Hugh then? We took on the term Singular too soon. We are still humans, live and think like humans in our worlds. He will be the first true Singular and then... well, no one can say.

For a terrible moment he reminded me of Viola and how her religion, her belief in a spiritual afterlife, had driven us apart. But that wasn't Hugh. This "ascension" that was happening was already underway. He felt it, he knew it, there was no faith involved.

"What about me?" I asked. I felt small and weak for saying it. I felt my face grow hot and heard the bass drumbeat of my heart pounding in my head. It was a selfish thought, but consciousness can be so very selfish. After all we had done, after as far as we had come, he was leaving me. Maybe it was time for me to be a bit selfish.

"We have some time," he said, gently taking my hand. It was all he could offer.

I considered refusing it, turning my back on him and leaving him before he could leave me. But I loved him in a way I hadn't imagined possible. I squeezed his hand and pulled him to me, wrapping my arms around him and holding him as tightly as I could for as long as I could.

Chapter Thirty-Three

"How long did you have?" Simon asked. We were back in that little red convertible, the greenery whipping past us as we headed to the spaceship that lay on the horizon at the edge of this world. After Doctor Kata, he had taken me back to the hotel and let me eat and sleep before our trip.

"Almost three years," I said, just loud enough for him to hear me over the wind. "But it wasn't enough."

Simon nodded but didn't reply. I turned and watched the lush green landscape whip by, let the hum of rubber on the road lull me.

Images of our final days flashed by. Making love to him, only to have him freeze in the middle of it. Long conversations we had at our kitchen table where he would whisper to me what his expanding sense of self felt like. Hikes on our desert world where he would become a statue and I would sit and wait until he came back, even if it took days or weeks.

Those days were precious and terrible at the same time.

When it finally happened, it was almost a relief.

"How did it happen?" Simon asked as if he had been reading my thoughts.

I shrugged. "It wasn't all that dramatic. It was at breakfast, Hugh with his toast and eggs again. A pile of yellow on the brown of the toast halfway to his mouth. He paused, that beatific look coming onto his face again. His freezes had become extreme and he wasn't with me that much anymore."

My eyes were dry, but I felt like I was crying. My throat clenched and my stomach roiled. My hand shook and I felt uncomfortable in the seat of the car. I took a deep breath and continued. "His eyes were distant, like he was a million miles away, but then they came into focus, those pools of pale blue pulling me in once again like they had so many times. 'It's time,' he said in French, his voice a husky whisper. 'I love you,' he added, and then…"

The land was flattening out and I could see the top of the ship on the eerily flat horizon. I didn't continue. The details didn't matter to me anymore. Hugh was gone, subsumed by the system, a part of everything around me, but apart from me.

I had told my story to Simon, and it was time for me to decide. Do I have something to live for or should I leave this world and erase myself?

———

BY THE TIME HUGH LEFT, I FELT NUMB TO THE PROCESS. MY lover was a statue more than he was a real presence in my life. And even when he was with me he was often confused, mentally, as if the input was just too much. The long, slow-motion loss of him had changed me. I was quiet and intro-verted. I didn't express much emotion. I didn't feel much at all.

After he told me he loved me—*je t'aime*, in French of course—he just disappeared, that little piece of toast with eggs stacked on it fell to the wooden table with a splat.

I didn't freak out. Like I said, time had changed me. I took a deep breath, letting out a long sigh, and cleaned up from breakfast.

I went about it slowly. Smelling the eggs and toast, scraping the remnants of our meals into the sink. Flicking the garbage disposal on and really enjoying the violent rumble of it. Running hot water on a washcloth and wiping down the smooth brown wood of the kitchen table.

And when it was done, I just stood there for the longest time, that damp washcloth in my hand. I didn't know what to do. I didn't know what there was left to do.

I didn't feel sad, not really. I didn't even feel confused. I just felt stuck. Like a leaf slowly rotating in the gentle eddy of a stream. Not going anywhere. Not changing.

I stood there for hours. My legs began to ache, but I didn't care. I got thirsty and then hungry, but it didn't matter. The sun went down and the stars came out and I stood there.

When Hugh was still with me, I always knew what to do. If he was frozen, I would wait for him to come back. If he was confused, I would keep him safe. If he wasn't frozen and coherent, I would be with him.

But now, he wasn't frozen or unfrozen, he was gone. Or… he was all around me. I didn't really understand. His consciousness had been subsumed by the system. Or maybe sublimated is a better word. He had ascended to a different kind of consciousness. One more primal and more expansive at the same time. He was the singularity.

When the sun came back up, it occurred to me that I was the one "frozen" now. And that was a thought I couldn't bear. So I walked back over to the sink and draped the now dry rag over the edge of it.

I then slowly walked to the portal and left my desert world. I went back to Level One. I erased my desert world, because it had become *our* desert world.

I can admit to feeling a sense of relief for a while. That the nightmare of his slow departure was over. But that relief came with an equal portion of guilt for even feeling it. After that came deep depression. After that I suspended myself for a year.

Chapter Thirty-Four

"That old saying, 'time heals all wounds,' is a lie," I told Simon. We were sitting on the grass of that eerily flat plain, the form of the Niña towering over us like some great metal cliff.

"What do you mean?" he asked.

We were going to visit the ship. I wanted to now, but I also wanted to finish the story. I kept thinking I was done, but then finding more to say. Simon had sensed this and taken me out into the plain and had continued to listen to my ramblings.

"Time doesn't really heal the wounds," I said. "Not completely. It just makes them more bearable. You don't get over a loss like this, you just become functional again."

Simon nodded. "Are you functional now?"

I laughed, it sounded tinny as it bounced off the metal ship towering over us. "I've spent much of the decades since Hugh died—ascended, whatever the hell he did—suspended. I haven't actually spent enough time conscious to let time make the wounds bearable."

"Maybe you just need something to do," Simon offered.

I smiled, I could feel it was one of those limp smiles like Hugh had given me when it became clear what was happening to him. I hated it and erased it with a frown. "The ethical quandary of this new transfer to biological is interesting," I said. "I will admit that much."

"And your suggestion?"

I shook my head. "You need to stop this, Simon." My voice was low but had an edge to it. "I don't believe you haven't already thought this through. I don't believe for a second that I am the only one capable of seeing the problems Singulars, and the Biologicals they create, could have. Doctor Kata's surprise, that she had never even thought of the dilemma, was *not* believable."

Simon pursed his lips and then nodded. "Very well. What do you want to know?"

I didn't answer right away. I had been waiting for this since I met Simon. Waiting for him to tell me who he was, what was really going on. But right then, everything seemed to slow down and I couldn't speak, I could only feel.

I felt the flat plain under me that I sat on. It was covered in a dense turf of short grass like a golf course. I smelled the greenness of it. I studied the Niña, her hull was a dark grey metal that was pitted and scarred, as if this simulation of it was showing her actual wear and tear.

I could hear Simon breathing and the gentlest of breezes on my face. The sun was beating down from a clear blue sky above me.

I could feel my heart beating and was thirsty again. My

biology was dense in this Level Ten world. It was insistent and never satisfied. It was constant and I was beginning to grow more used to it. I was beginning to like it.

The moment of silence stretched out, but finally it was over. "I want to know everything," I whispered.

He nodded. "But not here," he whispered back, just like Hugh had once.

"Where?"

"Before we headed out here the first time, I had promised you a place where you could see forever. I will tell you there."

Chapter Thirty-Five

AFTER HUGH LEFT, AFTER I SPENT ALL THAT TIME IN LEVEL One, after I suspended myself for a year, I tried to find a place for me.

I went from world to world to world. I had the kind of silly adventures that Ryan and I used to embark on. Climbing mountains. Rafting down rivers. Flying high above spectacular landscapes. In fact, Ryan was there with me at the start, but soon he couldn't stand my black moods and found other things to do.

It didn't mean anything to me anymore. I had done all that before things had gotten dangerous for us Singulars on Earth. I had done all that before I had work and purpose in this technological afterlife. I had done all that before Hugh.

It all felt hollow to me. None of it mattered and I knew it.

Without Hugh, I didn't matter.

I then descended into darker distractions. Pleasure worlds, simulated drugs, violent survival worlds. These more extreme experiences helped distract me. But they ended up feeling hollow too.

I went through rounds and rounds of this. I would try my best to find a place, to find meaning. I would fail, suspend myself for a year or ten, and then try again.

And every time as I sat in my white Level One World, I would find the Erase program that had been used against us by the Osiris Corporation so very long ago. I would sit there and ponder using it. Ask myself what eternity was worth without meaning.

Until this last time. I came out of suspension and started looking for a world to visit. That's when I found the world that I met Simon on. A world called "Home."

Home stood out when I was searching. It had over a third of our souls active in it. It had half of our system resources devoted to it. That curiosity had drawn me in.

———

"CAPTAIN ON THE DECK!" THE YOUNG MAN SHOUTED. HE snapped to attention and saluted me. I heard his cry echo down the long central corridor of the Niña.

I stood there blinking for a moment. I didn't recognize this man, but he obviously recognized me. I suspected this was Simon's doing, another attempt to remind me who I used to be.

He was dressed in a dull grey jumpsuit, and beside him was a spindly bot that echoed the man's movements, so it too was standing there stiffly, saluting me.

Not that the bot was really standing. It was about as tall as the man on a wheeled platform with four limbs with various tools on the end of each hand. This was a maintenance bot, the kind that roved the Niña, the Pinta, and the Santa Maria and did repairs and maintenance.

"Please don't," I said to the man. His forehead crinkled, his eyes going to Simon who gave him a small nod and then he relaxed. The robot relaxed too.

"Welcome aboard, sir," the young man said, his tone normal this time.

"You're operating that bot?" I asked.

"Yes, sir," he said, a tad too enthusiastically. "I feel privileged to serve such an important function."

Now my forehead crinkled. Things had changed. This Singular wasn't off gallivanting on some adventurous world, he was here operating a bot that could run by itself. "Why don't you let it run on auto?" I asked.

His forehead crinkled again. It was clear we were having trouble relating to each other. "Sir," he said, his voice serious, "what could be more important than taking care of the Niña? What could be more worthy of my attention and time?"

Depending on skill level and aptitude, I could easily think of many things, but I didn't say that. If this fellow wanted to spend his days operating a robot, so be it.

"Carry on," I said and turned to Simon who led me down the long corridor to the front of the ship.

We soon passed a young woman operating a robot. This one was doing a small weld on a bulkhead door. Once we were out of earshot of both of them, I asked, "Why do they spend their days doing something so mundane?"

Simon stopped, his foot scraping against the metal floor. "Mundane or not, it is work worth doing."

"But the bots could do it themselves," I said.

"We do it better. Surely you, of all people, see the worth of giving extra attention to our home."

It was a strange thought. Here on this world people chose to spend their days preparing simulated food for others to consume, or operating robots that didn't need operators, or sitting by the ocean painting a picture, or playing a simple game of chess.

It all seemed so banal. So beneath where we had come since leaving our biological lives. But my mind flipped over and suddenly I could see it. My life during the exodus from Earth had had meaning because I had had work worth doing. And after that, I had had Hugh, and that relationship was my "work." Since Hugh, I haven't had any work, or anything worth doing. Distracting myself is what was truly banal, not the work these Singulars were doing.

I smiled, it was a real smile this time. "I see," I said.

"This way," Simon said. "It's time for that view I promised you."

Chapter Thirty-Six

"THAT WAY IS EARTH." SIMON POINTED AT THE STAR FIELD THAT nearly surrounded us. We had walked the length of the ship until we ended up in what Simon called the "observatory." It was a small room with a tiny spiral staircase that led to this observation bubble on the tip of the Niña.

I knew the ship, and no such room existed, but it was a minor deviation from reality and totally worth it for the view. I imagine that many of the Singulars on this world come here to see the stars. To know where we are, where we have come from, and where we are going.

"And that is Alpha Centauri." Simon pointed down the length of the ship. There was a yellow glow at the far end of it and a bright star shining through it. The Niña was decelerating for our stop there, the aft end of the ship pointed towards our destination.

"How close are we?" I asked.

"Thirty-two years," Simon answered. "Close." He pointed

to the port. "That tiny dot there is the Pinta and to the starboard is the Santa Maria."

I slowly turned, taking in the vastness of space. The endless stars strewn across the black velvet void. I took a deep breath and let it slowly come out. Here was space. Here was the ultimate desert.

Since Hugh had left, I had gone anywhere but to a desert world. I was afraid that I wouldn't be able to handle it. That the dry feel of the desert would remind me too much of him and I wouldn't survive it. I know, that feeling would seem to be at odds with my suicidal tendencies, but I assure you it is not. What I wanted was escape from my pain, not to descend into it.

I spent a few more minutes enjoying the beauty of the stars, but the sound of Simon breathing, the smell of his breath as he stood so close to me, brought me back to his promise.

"Can you tell me now?" I asked.

He looked at me shyly and nodded. "It's a lot, though," he said.

"I'm ready," I lied.

"Just promise me you will hear me out until I have said everything."

I paused. Thoughts of him revealing to me that he was really Hugh, that he had fought his way back from his merge with the system, that he had been waiting for me to be ready for him. I felt angry at myself. I felt my face flush at the silliness of the thought and then I took a deep breath and tried to let go of that too. Of course, I wanted Hugh back. No matter how many centuries passed, I would always want my Hugh back.

"Just tell me, Simon."

He nodded, his eyes going towards Alpha Centauri before returning to mine. He was clearly nervous. "I don't know where to start," he said.

I nodded, thinking back over our time together. How he had found me when I came into this world. His claim to have become a Singular on our stop at Mars, although I had no memory of him. Pregnant Mrs. Tanner on her farm. Doctor Kata and the plan to transfer back to Biologicals. The kid climbing in the tree when I first entered Home. How there always seemed to be something different about him.

It clicked in my mind and I blurted it out. "You are not a Singular, are you?"

He pursed his lips and slowly shook his head.

"You were 'born' here, weren't you?"

"I was the first of us," he said slowly, each word clearly articulated.

"Who are your parents?" I asked.

Simon paused and looked away, looking again across the length of the ship towards our destination. I could see real fear on his face. He was afraid of what would happen if he told me. But why would he fear that? Who could his parents possibly be that would cause me to react?

And then it hit me… And then he said it…

"Hugh is my father," he said, still looking away from me.

My knees went weak and I leaned against the clear bubble of this room. The stars seemed to spin around me.

"And so are you," he said it so quietly I wasn't sure I had heard him right.

Chapter Thirty-Seven

Do we ever really know the people we love? Did I truly know Viola or Hugh or Simon?

I was alone in the observation bubble of the Niña, the planet Phaeton large, filling up the view instead of the stars that had been there for so many years.

The earth-ish planet had been dubbed Phaeton—a mythical planet that had once been thought to orbit between Mars and Jupiter. It was not, though, habitable, its atmosphere had too much hydrogen sulfide and carbon dioxide, not enough oxygen.

Thirty-two years had passed since Simon had told me he was the son of Hugh and me. Since he had explained how Hugh had created him and this world in the last few years of his life. How Simon had grown up here raised by several constructs and mentored by Hugh via holo videos he had prepared before his ascension into the system.

I had come to the world Home looking for a reason to live.

The journey of us Singulars back to Biological was that. A son was that. A piece of Hugh that I could interact with was that.

I had stayed on Home with Simon. I hadn't ever left. I had slowly become used to living again.

The clank of footfalls on the spiral staircase behind me drew my mind back to the present. There was work to be done.

"It's time, Father," Simon said, a smile on his old face. We all aged here, and Simon with his white hair and wrinkled face looked to be in his seventies. He was a robust and hearty seventy, but seventy nonetheless.

I nodded, turning away from the planet and looking back out at the desert of the stars, indulging myself for a moment. I took a deep breath and slowly let it out. There was much work to do here at Alpha Centauri. We were transferring a few colonists, creating new Singulars. We wanted to do some mining on the asteroid belt, we badly needed to replenish some of our supplies. We had trading to do and technology to exchange with these people, these Biologicals.

Earth was a long way behind us, but we remembered how the Biologicals there treated us, how they feared us. Many had wanted to skip the stop entirely, but it wasn't practical, and it wasn't healthy for us to be so isolated. We still needed more consciousnesses, we still had so much more to learn.

I turned with a sigh and followed Simon down the stairs. My knees and my knuckles ached, I too was an old man. I had come to appreciate the "reality" of it. It kept me grounded.

I followed Simon down a corridor and through a bulkhead into the bridge of the Niña.

"Captain on the deck," a young man shouted with a crisp salute that was echoed by the other five people there.

"At ease," I said.

This bridge, like the observation bubble, was another deviation from reality, but it made our work here more "real." Although, one day, we might have to build a real bridge that could be manned by real Biologicals.

Doctor Kata and her team had not perfected the technology yet, but she was getting close. We still lacked areas on our ship that could support biological life. That was one of the things we needed to trade for.

"The governor is hailing us," the communications officer said from her seat.

"Put her on the big screen," I said.

She nodded and the view of Phaeton was replaced by the wrinkled face of Helen Konter, the governor of the colony.

"Good morning, Helen," I said with a smile. We had spoken many times along the journey towards her. I think it had helped that I had grown old over the years just as she had. She was an elegant woman with her white hair pulled up into a neat bun.

"Welcome to Phaeton Colony, Paul," she said with a smile. "We are glad you are finally here."

"As are we," I said.

Simon was standing beside me, I didn't look at him, but out of the corner of my eye I could see him smiling. I won't lie to you, I still miss Hugh every single day, but I have found that Simon fills a place in my heart that I had long since forgotten about. He is my son and I love him fiercely. His habits that remind me of Hugh no longer hurt, but delight me.

We are both planning to transfer to Biological once Dr. Kata and her team succeeds. Once we find a planet we can call home. It will be my last transfer. I have seen forever, and just like Viola and Hugh, it's not for me.

"Shall we get to work?" Helen asked, looking from me to Simon and back to me.

"Let's. There is so much to do."

Afterword

Stories fool me, all the time. This one for sure. When I wrote this and edited it, I was sure it was 100% stand-alone, no sequel, no way. Now that I'm getting it ready to leave the nest, I have a few whispers of ideas, just intriguing little "what if's" that could take the story further. It would be a different kind of book, for sure, but the possibilities are there.

What about you? Are you curious what is next for Paul, Simon, and the Singulars? If so, please let me know. There are tons of ways to reach out. Write a review wherever you buy books. Go to my website, robertjmccarter.com, and fill out the contact page. I'm on twitter at @robertjmccarter, and you can join my facebook group at: www.facebook.com/groups/robertjmccarter.

Some stories fool you more than others, and it's often good not knowing what's going to be involved when you foolishly set off on a creative endeavor. I was so fooled by this story, that when I started writing, I thought I was writing another short story along the vein of "A Postscript for Elizabeth," "The Turing Test Will Be Televised," and especially "One Core, One Consciousness." Stories that look at non-biological, formerly human consciousnesses. Something that my subconscious has been interested in for a while.

But then as I wrote, a mystery developed, the world got deep and complicated, and the story spun forth in the most delightful way. The story became a novel (albeit a short one) and I happily typed along wanting to know how it ended, wanting to find out who Simon was, wanting to know how Paul would end up thinking about forever.

(And yes, I really do write stories, even novels, having no idea what the end is. It's part of the journey and the fun of the process for me. I follow along, much like a reader. In this case, Simon wasn't who I thought he first was, much to the betterment of the story.)

This changed from "one" of my stories about non-biological consciousness to "the" story about non-biological, formerly human consciousness. Love and loss in a post-biological existence.

I've written a lot of novels and stories featuring ghosts, and in many ways, this is the science fiction mirror to that and asks a lot of the same questions. What makes a life worth living, even if that life is not flesh and blood? What makes a life real? What matters when we are released from the constraints of a biological life?

So a surprise, but one I am very grateful for.

If you are so motivated, please do reach out. I'm listening. Your voice matters. I'd love to hear what you think.

Acknowledgments

Unlike *Of Things Not Seen*, my last novel, this book was easy to write—although it was delayed by the same personal tribulations as that book. That doesn't say I wasn't helped along a lot, so time for those "thank yous":

Gratitude to my beta readers, John Bifano, Roni Hornstein, Aleia O'Reilly, Eliot Schipper, and Janine Schipper. Extra thanks to Janine whose cogent questions helped me clarify some core concepts. And forever thanks to my amazing wife Aleia who let me read this book to her twice so I could hear it and catch a lot of goofs.

Big thanks to Elizabeth Fitzekam, for her enthusiasm, thoroughness, and diligence in helping me get this book out the door for you all to read.

As always, much gratitude to Diana Cox for her excellent proofreading that makes me look good (*www.novelproofreading.com*).

And thank you, dear reader, I hope you enjoyed the journey. All stories need a home, need an audience, and I'm so glad you gave some of your precious time to this one. If you're interested in those other stories I mentioned in the afterword, all three (and seven more) are collected in *Life After: Stories of Life, Death, and the Places in Between.*

About the Author

Robert J. McCarter is the author of six novels, three novellas, and dozens of short stories. He is a finalist for the *Writers of the Future* contest and his stories have appeared in *The Saturday Evening Post, Adomeda Spaceways Inflight Magazine, Everyday Fiction,* and numerous anthologies. His short stories have been published alongside such luminaries as Brandon Sanderson, Peter S. Beagle, Jody Lynn Nye, and David Farland.

He has written a series of first person ghost novels (starting with *Shuffled Off: A Ghost's Memoir*) and a superhero / love story series (*Neutrinoman and Lightningirl: A Love Story*). Ten of his short stories were published in *Life After: Stories of Life, Death, and the Places in Between.*

He lives in the mountains of Arizona with his amazing wife and his ridiculously adorable dog.

Find out more at:
robertjmccarter.com

facebook.com/robertjmccarter

twitter.com/RobertJMcCarter

instagram.com/robert.j.mccarter

Books by Robert J. McCarter

Novels in the "Ghost's Memoir" world:

- Shuffled Off: A Ghost's Memoir, Book 1
- Drawing the Dead
- To Be a Fool: A Ghost's Memoir, Book 2
- Of Things Not Seen: A Ghost's Memoir, Book 3

Other Novels:

- Seeing Forever

Books in the Neutrinoman and Lightningirl Series:

- Meteor Attack! Lightningirl and Neutrinoman, A Love Story. Episode 1
- Toxic Asset: Lightningirl and Neutrinoman, A Love Story. Episode 2
- Protocol X: Lightningirl and Neutrinoman, A Love Story. Episode 3
- Season 1 (Omnibus edition of Episodes 1 - 3)
- Off Book: Lightningirl and Neutrinoman, A Love Story. Episode 4 (*Coming soon*)

Short Stores and Collections

- Life After: Stories of Life, Death, and the Places in Between
- Probability: Resolve
- The Turing Test Will Be Televised
- Ghost Hacker, Zombie Maker

For a complete list, go to RobertJMcCarter.com

CPSIA information can be obtained
at www.ICGtesting.com
Printed in the USA
LVOW11s1815090518
576571LV00002B/402/P